What had come over him?

Jack swallowed hard as Alayna's soft protest echoed around him. He opened his hand and looked at his palm, still feeling the warmth, the softness of her breast.

He closed his hand into a fist, his lips thinning. He didn't want to get involved with her. Even less, to hurt her. She was an angel. A woman who deserved a man who was willing to give her the children that she wanted so desperately.

"I'm sorry," he mumbled. "I—" But he couldn't think of an explanation for his actions—nothing but the truth, which was that he wanted her. Needed her. He yearned for her softness, her compassion.

But what did he have to give her in return?

Jack pushed himself to his feet. He strode down the pier, the weathered planks pitching beneath his feet as he all but ran from her. From temptation.

From himself.

From memories that haunted him.

Dear Reader,

The joys of summer are upon us—along with some July fireworks from Silhouette Desire!

The always wonderful Jennifer Greene presents our July MAN OF THE MONTH in *Prince Charming's Child*. A contemporary romance version of *Sleeping Beauty*, this title also launches the author's new miniseries, HAPPILY EVER AFTER, inspired by those magical fairy tales we loved in childhood. And ever-talented Anne Marie Winston is back with a highly emotional reunion romance in *Lovers' Reunion*. The popular miniseries TEXAS BRIDES by Peggy Moreland continues with the provocative story of *That McCloud Woman*. Sheiks abound in Judith McWilliams's *The Sheik's Secret*, while a plain Jane is wooed by a millionaire in Jan Hudson's *Plain Jane's Texan*. And Barbara McCauley's new dramatic miniseries, SECRETS!, debuts this month with *Blackhawk's Sweet Revenge*.

We've got more excitement for you next month—watch for the premiere of the compelling new Desire miniseries THE TEXAS CATTLEMAN'S CLUB. Some of the sexiest, most powerful men in the Lone Star State are members of this prestigious club, and they all find love when they least expect it! You'll learn more about THE TEXAS CATTLEMAN'S CLUB in our August Dear Reader letter, along with an update on Silhouette's new continuity, THE FORTUNES OF TEXAS, debuting next month.

And this month, join in the celebrations by treating yourself to all six passionate Silhouette Desire titles.

Enjoy!

Joan Marlow Golan
Senior Editor, Silhouette Desire

Please address questions and book requests to:
Silhouette Reader Service
U.S.: 3010 Walden Ave., P.O. Box 1325, Buffalo, NY 14269
Canadian: P.O. Box 609, Fort Erie, Ont. L2A 5X3

THAT McCLOUD WOMAN
WOMAN
PEGGY MORELAND

SILHOUETTE *Desire*®
Published by Silhouette Books
America's Publisher of Contemporary Romance

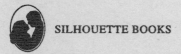

SILHOUETTE BOOKS

ISBN 0-373-76227-5

THAT McCLOUD WOMAN

Visit us at www.romance.net

Printed in U.S.A.

Books by Peggy Moreland

Silhouette Desire

A Little Bit Country #515
Run for the Roses #598
Miss Prim #682
The Rescuer #765
Seven Year Itch #837
The Baby Doctor #867
Miss Lizzy's Legacy #921
A Willful Marriage #1024
*Marry Me, Cowboy #1084
*A Little Texas Two-Step #1090
*Lone Star Kind of Man #1096
†*The Rancher's Spitting' Image* #1156
†*The Restless Virgin* #1163
†*A Sparkle in the Cowboy's Eyes* #1168
†*That McCloud Woman* #1227

Silhouette Special Edition

Rugrats and Rawhide #1084

*Trouble in Texas
†Texas Brides

PEGGY MORELAND

published her first romance with Silhouette in 1989. She's a natural storyteller, with a sense of humor that will tickle your fancy, and Peggy's goal is to write a story that readers will remember long after the last page is turned. Winner of the 1992 National Readers' Choice Award, the 1997 Golden Quill Award, and a 1994 RITA finalist, Peggy frequently appears on bestseller lists around the country. A native Texan, she and her family live in Round Rock, Texas.

To my college roomies, Melissa Gerland Dillard, Brenda Bryant Medlin and Cyndi Lumpkin Clanton. In spite of the miles and the years, you are all still cherished friends.

One

With nowhere to go, and in no hurry to get there, Jack Cordell dumped a second spoonful of sugar into his coffee and slowly stirred, killing time.

The town he'd stopped in for lunch was a small one, the diner he'd chosen a mom and pop type place that boasted home-style cooking and a blue plate special for $4.95. Though the price of the food mattered little to Jack, the appeal of a home-cooked meal did. After six months on the road, eating cardboard-flavored food, his stomach had been ready for something with a little sustenance to it.

Though crowded and noisy when he'd first arrived, the diner was nearly empty now, the only sound the rattle of pans from the kitchen and the occasional squeak of the waitress's crepe-soled shoes on the worn linoleum as she went about her duties, clearing off tables after the noon rush. The woman looked to be on the downhill side of fifty, full breasted, thick waisted and with a tongue as sharp as the pencil tucked behind her ear. She wore her hair piled high on top of her head, a metallic gold clamp of some sort holding her bottle-red hair in place. She worked with an efficiency of movement that said she was an old hand at slinging hash.

The dusty plate-glass window on Jack's right offered him a bird's-eye view of the diner's empty parking lot, the bank across the street and the post office beside it. With a slight turn of his head, he had a clear shot of the entire downtown area. All two blocks of it. Though he'd spent the last five years in Houston and was accustomed to its towering skyline and traffic-clogged expressways, Jack had grown up in a town about the size of Driftwood, and found the small town appealing, almost peaceful.

And it had been a long time since Jack had known any peace.

As he stared at the big, lazy-branched oak that shaded the bank's entrance, a weariness settled on his shoulders. He was tired of running. Tired of living out of his truck, eating his meals out of grease-stained paper sacks. Tired of the monotony of chasing a white line, his only companion a fifth of whiskey he kept tucked underneath the front seat, while he tried to outrun his guilt, his grief—and when he couldn't outrun it, drown it. Neither seemed to work. The guilt still weighed heavily on him, the grief a cancer eating away at what remained of his heart.

He knew he had a home to go to, a business to tend. But the idea of returning to either held no appeal. Not anymore.

As he stared at the big oak, his thoughts bluer than blue, his heart a lead weight in his chest, a woman stepped from the bank's double doors and started across the street. She was a petite little thing, fragile looking.

The thick mane of white-blond hair that hung just past her shoulders only added to that fragility. She wore a long, sleeveless dress of the palest blue that hit her about midcalf. One of those shapeless dresses that didn't offer a clue to the figure beneath. Thin-strapped sandals, though, exposed small, slender feet, and a hint that the rest of her might be similarly proportioned.

With her chin dipped down, he didn't have a clear view of her face, but he couldn't help but notice the way she walked—kind of slowlike, her posture that of a person lost in deep contemplation. As he watched, a sigh seemed to move through her and she lifted her head, squaring her shoulders. At the same time, her steps quickened, bringing her closer to the diner and the window he watched her through.

He focused on her face and was struck by the oddest sensation. It was like looking into the face of an angel. A sexy-looking angel, without question, but an angel, nonetheless. Creamy, smooth complexion. Delicate features almost too perfect to be real. Bright, clear blue eyes. Full, moist lips. An innate sexuality in her movements stirred parts of his body that he was sure had died on the vine months ago.

He lost sight of her as she skipped up the steps to the diner, and he quickly shifted his gaze to the door, waiting for her to step inside. She pushed her way through the entrance, bringing a blast of hot, humid air with her. She paused, glancing around, and met his gaze for the briefest of seconds. When she did, the sweetest, yet most sensual smile touched her lips before she turned away and headed for the counter.

She brushed damp hair from her forehead. "Maudie," he heard her say, "I sure hope you saved me a tall glass of that lime iced tea you're so famous for."

The waitress caught up her apron to wipe her hands, her carmine-painted lips splitting in a welcoming smile. "Thirsty, are you?"

"Parched." The sexy angel—as Jack had already started to think of her—sank down onto a stool at the counter, her dress settling like a billowy cloud around her legs. She propped an elbow on the counter and fanned her face with a delicately boned hand. "I swear, it's hot enough out there to fry eggs on the sidewalk."

Maudie shoveled a scoop of ice into a glass. "Did you hear that, Ed?" she yelled through the pass-through window that opened to the kitchen. She hefted an aluminum pitcher and poured tea into the glass without spilling a drop. "Alayna says we could fry eggs on the sidewalk. Why don't you turn off the grill and move your cookin' outside? It'd sure cool things off in here. Might even save us some money on gas."

Jack heard a gruff, male voice, but couldn't make out the man's reply. Alayna—thanks to Maudie, he now had a name to associate with the sexy angel—touched her fingertips to her chest and batted her eyes at the man on the other side of the window. Her voice all but dripped southern honey as she replied, "My-y, oh my-y, Ed, but you do-o-o know how to turn a woman's head with your sweet talk."

Maudie tossed back her head and hooted at the ceiling. "Alayna, I'll swear, for a minute there, you sounded just like your mother." She shook her head, still chuckling, as she pulled up a stool on the opposite side of the counter. "How's the old bat doin', anyway?"

Alayna didn't even flinch at the verbal slur to her mother. "Fine. Giving Daddy heck, as usual."

"Serves him right for goin' off and marryin' a Southern Belle and abandoning his home state of Texas."

Maudie shook her head regretfully as she picked up a glass to polish, obviously preparing to settle in for a long gossip. "So how's the remodelin' comin' along?"

Her smile fading a bit, Alayna took a sip of tea, then set the glass down and plucked a napkin from the chrome dispenser on the counter. "Not very well, I'm afraid." She dabbed at the corners of her mouth—a definite stall tactic in Jack's estimation—then frowned, wadding the napkin in her fist. "Frank left."

Maudie's eyes widened, then narrowed. "How much did he take you for?"

Jack watched Alayna's cheeks turn an engaging shade of pink, before she lifted her glass as if to hide behind it. "Enough," he heard her murmur.

Maudie slapped the counter hard enough to make the napkin dispenser rock and Alayna jump a good two inches off the stool. "That no-count drifter. I knew he'd end up scammin' you. Didn't I tell you that you couldn't trust that polecat?"

Alayna's cheeks pinkened even more, but whether from embarrassment or in defiance, Jack wasn't sure.

"Yes, you did," he heard her reply. "But I had little choice but to hire him. He was the only man in town with the skills necessary to remodel the Pond House for me and the only one who was willing to take on the job."

"Humph! I guess so. The name McCloud would be temptin' enough for a double-dealin' snake like Frank, but with you wearin' the title of doctor, too, I'm sure he saw nothin' but deep pockets and a chance for some easy money."

A doctor, huh? Jack knew he was eavesdropping, but couldn't seem to work up the good manners required to block out the conversation. And now he had a last name to attach to the woman. Alayna McCloud. He liked the sound of it. Soft and feminine, but with an underlying strength. Much like his impression of the woman.

He shook his head with regret as he digested what he'd heard. So she'd been scammed by a remodeler? It wouldn't be the first time he'd heard of that happening.

"He did make the house livable," he heard her say in the man's defense. "And the kitchen and two of the bathrooms are at least functional."

"And I suppose you paid him up-front?"

"Well," she began evasively, "not all of it. Besides, he said he needed the money to pay his rent or his landlord was going to kick him and his family out on the street."

"Landsakes, Alayna! Frank doesn't have any family. You let that man work on your heartstrings while he shoulda' been workin' on your house." Alayna's chin snapped up at the criticism and Maudie sighed heavily. "So what are you going to do now?"

Alayna glanced down at the counter and dipped her finger in the condensation the glass had left there, her brow furrowing. "I thought I might run an ad in the Austin paper." She lifted her face, her eyes so full of innocence and hope that Jack felt the need to put a fist in the face of the man who'd cheated her. "Do you think there might be a carpenter there in need of a job?"

Jack's ears perked up at the word "carpenter" and an itch jumped to life on his palms. He rubbed his hands along his thighs to ease it. It had been years since he'd swung a hammer, worked a lathe, felt the satisfaction of wood warming beneath his hands. Uncovering the grain in a piece of painted wood, pumping blood back into an old house. He was a carpenter by trade, but all he'd done for the last couple of years was push papers, put out fires, haggle with subcontractors and inspectors. Did he really want to go back to that? Did he even want to go back to Houston at all?

He glanced out the window at the big oak with its barrel-size trunk and sprawling branches. He squinted his eyes and looked farther, taking note of the quiet street and the quaint shops that lined both sides. He'd grown up in a town like this, before moving to Houston. Small. Friendly. Where everybody knew everybody…and their business.

A sigh moved through him and he pushed back the memories before they could fully form. He was tired of running, but he wasn't ready to go back to Houston. Not yet. Maybe never.

Standing, he fished a couple of dollars out of his pocket and tossed them on the table, then scraped his cap from the seat and his ticket from the scarred Formica tabletop where Maudie had left it earlier. Crossing to the register, he dropped the ticket on the counter and worked his wallet from his back pocket.

Maudie aimed one last frown of disapproval in Alayna's direction, then stood and shifted to the register, pasting a smile on her face for Jack's benefit. "Was everythin' all right?" she asked as she punched the total into the register and took the ten-dollar bill he offered her.

"Fine, thank you," Jack murmured politely as he accepted his change. "Much obliged." Stuffing his wallet back into his pocket, he glanced one last time in Alayna's direction, then turned and left the diner.

Alayna let the door to the diner close behind her, then stopped, drawing in a deep breath. Well, she'd expected an "I told you so" from Maudie, and she'd certainly gotten it. Not that it changed anything. She was still out

several thousand dollars and left with a half-finished remodeling job.

Things could be worse, she told herself, looking for
the bright side of the situation as she started down the
steps. Frank could have taken her money and skipped out
on her before he'd made the house livable again. She
could at least be thankful for that. After all, she was able
to sleep and bathe in her own house, which was, in her
opinion, a definite step in the right direction. She could
even cook her own meals and no longer needed to take
advantage of her cousins' hospitality. Though she had
enjoyed sharing her meals with Mandy, Sam and Merideth in their respective homes, and getting to know their
families, the time saved in traveling to and fro gave her
the opportunity to tackle other projects. She supposed she
had *that* to be thankful for, as well.

And there were the—

"Excuse me, ma'am."

Alayna jumped, sucking in a startled breath as a man
stepped from the shadow of the diner, blocking her path.

"I'm sorry," he mumbled, whipping off his cap and
dipping his chin to his chest in apology. "I didn't mean
to scare you."

Alayna pressed a hand over her heart to still its frantic
beating. "You didn't frighten me."

He glanced up, one thick brow arched high over a
doubtful eye as he nodded toward the hand she still
clutched at her chest. "Could have fooled me."

Alayna looked down at her hand, unaware that she had
even raised it, then dropped it to her side in embarrassment. She laughed self-consciously as she lifted her gaze
to the man's again. She relaxed a little when she found
nothing threatening in his eyes or in his stance. "Well,
maybe just a little," she admitted. She cocked her head,

eyeing him curiously. "You were in the diner earlier, weren't you?"

He took his cap in both hands, curling and uncurling its bill. "Yea, ma'am, I was. And I couldn't help overhearing your conversation."

Alayna wrinkled her nose. "You mean Maudie's lecture."

He shrugged. "Sounded as if she had your best interest at heart."

She rolled her eyes, then sighed. "Yes, I suppose, though I feel rather foolish. Especially since Maudie warned me about Frank." She angled her head, frowning just a little. "I don't believe I've seen you around before. Do you live in Driftwood?"

"Oh, no, ma'am," he answered with a quick shake of his head. "I'm not from around here."

"I didn't think so." She laughed. "In a town the size of Driftwood, everyone pretty much knows everyone else—and their business," she added sagely.

Jack frowned upon hearing her echo his own sentiments about the town, but he was at a loss as how to approach her with the idea that had come upon him earlier as he'd stared out the window at the quiet street. He dropped his hands to his sides and tapped his cap nervously against his thigh.

Alayna continued to peer at him. "Is there something I can do for you?" she asked helpfully.

"Well, yes, ma'am, there is," he began uncertainly. "I couldn't help overhearing your conversation, and you mentioning that you were going to advertise for someone to complete your remodeling job. I'd like to apply for the job, if you'll allow me, and save you the trouble of posting an ad."

Alayna's eyes sharpened in interest. "Oh? Are you a carpenter?"

"Yes, ma'am. I've worked in carpentry most of my life. My dad was a carpenter, and he taught me and my brother the trade. I can handle pretty much any job that pops up in a redo. Electrical. Plumbing. Painting. You name it." He snorted what might pass as a laugh. "I guess you could call me a jack-of-all-trades."

Intrigued, Alayna studied him. He was close to her age, maybe a bit older, with strong features, and broad shoulders. Definitely fit enough for the work that would be required of him. She liked to think she was an excellent judge of character and could tell a lot about a person by simply looking into their eyes. That he could meet her gaze squarely attested to his honesty in Alayna's estimation.

Yet, there was something in his eyes—or rather lacking in them—that concerned her. There was a sadness, an almost emptiness to the brown depths. Not that that would affect her decision to hire him. It simply intrigued her. There was a story there, a loss or disappointment of some kind that had left him disillusioned and withdrawn. She wondered if he'd share it with her, and wondered further if she could help him deal with it.

She gave herself a firm shake, forcing her mind to the situation at hand and her heart from the swell of sympathy she felt building.

She knew Maudie would throw a screaming fit if she discovered that Alayna was considering hiring a complete stranger right off the street, especially after the fiasco with Frank. But Alayna was desperate. She had to find someone to finish the job Frank had started.

"I pay by the hour, not the job," she said, then named a figure, watching his reaction.

He lifted a shoulder. "That's fine by me."

"And I handle the purchase of supplies."

"Whatever suits you."

"You said you weren't from around here."

"No, ma'am, I'm not."

"Then, where would you live?"

He pursed his lips thoughtfully, then shrugged. "I don't know. But I'm sure I could find a place."

She glanced away, looking down the street and away from him. "There's a small cabin on my property," she said thoughtfully. "I lived there until Frank made the house habitable."

Since she'd offered the information as a statement and not an invitation, Jack wasn't sure what kind of response she expected from him, so he remained silent.

"I suppose you could stay there," she said, turning her gaze back to him. "It isn't much, but it offers the essentials."

"I'm used to making do."

"Are you a man of your word?"

His chest swelled as if in asking the question she'd insulted him. "My word's as good as any legal contract you could have drawn."

"And I have your word that you'll see this remodeling job through to its end?"

He gave his chin a tight jerk of assent. "You have my word. I'll see the job done."

"When can you start?"

"When do you want me?"

She arched a brow, a smile teasing one corner of her mouth. "What are your plans for this afternoon?"

Jack shrugged. "Nothing in particular."

She quickly dug pen and paper from her purse, then turned the bag over, bracing it against her stomach while she used its side for a writing surface. "I have a few more errands to run," she told him as she jotted down directions to her house, "but I should be home by three."

She held out the slip of paper and Jack took it, studying her neat handwriting. When he glanced up, he saw that her hand was extended toward him. Along with it she offered him a smile. "I'm Alayna McCloud."

Up close, he found her eyes an even deeper blue than he'd thought before, and he quickly decided that a man could probably drown in their depths if he cared to look long and deeply enough. Thankfully Jack didn't. He took her hand, if a bit reluctantly, and shook it. "Jack Cordell."

Her smile broadened, dimples winking at him from her cheeks. She added a squeeze to the shake. "I'm pleased to meet you, Jack."

The warmth of her hand slowly worked its way up his arm while the added pressure in her grip seemed to draw his insides into a knot. Frowning, he uncurled his fingers from around hers and dropped his hand to his side, slowly flexing his fingers. "Same goes," he murmured, then abruptly turned away.

Jack sat on the porch steps, waiting...and slowly melting. He shoved his cap back on his head and used his shirtsleeve to mop the sweat from his brow. She'd said three, and it was already almost half past.

On a sigh, he stretched out his legs and tucked his pressed hands between his thighs, hunching his shoulders forward. Had he been too hasty in taking on this job? he asked himself. Was it the job itself that had appealed to him, the chance to work with his hands again? Or had it been the woman? It had been a long time since a woman had caught his attention enough to make him look twice. Even longer since he'd worked with his hands.

Maybe it was a mixture of the two, he decided, squinting his eyes thoughtfully as he stared out at the drive that led to the house. He gave his shoulder a lift, then shook his head. Didn't matter, he told himself. Either way, he had a job to do, a place to stay for a while. And a pretty woman to look at. Not a bad deal all the way around, no matter which way he looked at it.

While he was pondering all this, a cat slipped from beneath the porch steps and wound its way around his feet. Jack scowled at the scraggly-looking cat and nudged it away with the toe of his boot. At the sound of an engine, he glanced up, standing when he saw a minivan coming up the long drive. It stopped at an angle in front of the picket fence that surrounded the house, and Alayna slipped from behind the wheel and to the ground. She quickly ducked back inside, stretching to grab a sack of groceries from the passenger seat. With the movement, the hem of her dress rose, exposing a tanned calf, then the tender flesh behind her knee. At the sight, Jack felt his pulse kick and heat crawl up his neck.

"Hi!" she called brightly as she turned and headed toward him. "Sorry I'm late."

Jack frowned, tugging the bill of his cap low over his forehead as if to hide the truth of where his eyes had strayed. "No problem."

She stooped to give the cat that greeted her a loving pat. "I see you met Captain Jinx."

Jack's frown deepened as he watched the flea-bitten, stump-tailed cat arch beneath her hand, purring its contentment. "Yeah."

She straightened, lifting her gaze to his, a teasing smile

curving her lips when she saw the look of disgust on his face. "You don't like cats?"

He lifted a shoulder. "They're okay."

She laughed softly as she shifted the sack of groceries to her hip, then looked back down at the cat. "He's not really mine. He just appeared one day and stayed."

"Did you feed him?"

Alayna glanced up, her forehead wrinkling at the unexpected question. "Well, yes. As a matter of fact, I did. Why do you ask?"

He lifted a shoulder again. "That would be enough to convince him to stay."

Alayna stared at Jack a moment, caught once again by the sadness in his eyes, the emptiness there, wondering what had robbed them of their life, their sparkle. She wondered, too, if she fed Jack, as she had the cat, would he stay long enough to finish her remodeling job?

At the outrageousness of the thought, she shifted the sack of groceries in her arms. "What would you like to see first? The cabin where you'll be staying, or the house?"

Jack glanced over his shoulder toward the house. He didn't care one way or the other about his own accommodations. But the house and its distinct architecture had intrigued him from the moment he'd first caught sight of it. "The house, if you don't mind."

"The house, it is." Alayna led the way, with Jack following. When they reached the kitchen door, she juggled sack and purse, and he quickly stretched an arm in front of her, caught the screen door handle and pulled it open. "Thank you," she said, offering him a grateful smile as she passed by him.

Feeling the warmth of her smile and catching a whiff of the flowery scent that trailed her, Jack stared after her a second, watching the subtle movement of her hips beneath the sacklike dress, and the rhythmic sway of her hair across her shoulders and back. He wondered what the texture of her hair would feel like between his fingers, what she'd taste like when aroused. When he realized where his thoughts were taking him, he frowned and quickly stepped inside, letting the door close quietly behind him.

In the kitchen, Alayna set the bag of groceries on the counter, then began to dig out the items that needed refrigeration. "Would you like something to drink?" she asked, crossing to the refrigerator. "I made lemonade this morning, or I might be able to scare up a beer. Frank might have left one or two behind."

Jack looked around the kitchen, admiring the old glass-front cabinetry. "Lemonade's fine," he murmured absently. He crossed to the breakfast nook, tucked into a bay window, and ran his hand across the faded wallpaper, letting his fingers tell him the wall's history.

Alayna watched him as she pulled the pitcher of lemonade from the refrigerator. "Frank didn't do much in there," she offered. "My first priorities were the kitchen, my bedroom and bath." She took two glasses from the cabinet and filled them with ice.

"There's beaded paneling beneath this paper."

In the midst of pouring lemonade, Alayna glanced Jack's way and saw that he had pulled a knife from his pocket and was carefully scraping at the paper near the window frame. "What?" she asked, wondering what he was doing.

He folded the knife and stuck it back in his pocket. "Wood," he explained, plucking with a fingernail at the paper he'd loosened. Then added, "Two-inch tongue and groove.'' He gave his head a regretful shake. ''Somebody papered over solid wood walls.''

Intrigued, Alayna caught up their drinks and crossed to him. She offered him a glass, which Jack took, then she leaned to peer closely at the spot of wood he'd uncovered. ''Is that bad?'' she asked in concern.

The heat and intimacy of her body pressed against his had Jack sidestepping away from her, giving her room and himself the opportunity to breathe a little easier. ''Not necessarily bad. Just stupid.''

Alayna choked back a laugh upon hearing her ancestors referred to as ''stupid.'' The McClouds were a proud bunch, and probably wouldn't think kindly of a man who questioned their intelligence. She took a sip of her lemonade. ''So what do you propose we do about it?''

Jack turned his head to look at her, surprised by the ''we'' in her statement, but decided to take it as a sign that she trusted his opinion. ''It's your house. But if it was left up to me, I'd rip that paper off and let the wood breathe. It'd be a pretty sight, I can promise you that.''

Alayna looked at him, surprised by the level of emotion in his voice, his passion for something as innocuous as a wall of wood. ''Will it cost much?''

He lifted a shoulder, which seemed to be his favored means of communicating with her. ''Elbow grease, mainly. 'Course you never know what problems you might find when you start uncovering things.''

Alayna turned to look at the wall again, trying to imagine it without the faded paper, and wondering, too, what other things she would discover that Jack felt passionate about...and she *would* find out. There was still life inside him. The emotion he'd just displayed over her breakfast room wall proved that. ''Okay,'' she said, with a decisive nod at the faded paper, then turned to smile at him. "Let's do it."

"Now?"

Alayna laughed at the shocked look on his face, her blue eyes twinkling merrily. "No, not *now*, as in right this minute." She turned to look at the wall again, her smile softening. "But I think you're right. That wood needs to breathe."

That she would accept his advice so readily both surprised and relieved Jack. He knew from experience that homeowners could be a pain in the butt to work with, having ideas and opinions on how repairs should be made that could drive a remodeler straight up the wall. He just hoped that when he stripped off that paper, he didn't discover that it had been hung to cover up some problem, like termite or water damage. While he was thinking this, he felt a featherlight touch on his arm, then it was gone and Alayna was turning away, saying, "Come on. I'll show you the rest of the house."

Jack followed her, unconsciously rubbing a hand at the tingling sensation she'd left on his arm.

"The fireplace in the living room was sealed off years ago," she explained as she led the way to the front of the house. "I'd planned to open it and make it functional again." She paused in the archway that opened to the large living room. Jack stopped beside her, stealing a glance her way, and saw that she had her arms hugged up beneath her breasts in an oddly protective way. "But I'm afraid," she said with a disappointed sigh, "that this is one of the luxuries I'm going to have to forego in order to stay on budget."

Jack turned his head to follow her gaze...and the craftsman in him all but drooled at the sight before him. A huge limestone fireplace dominated the opposite wall, its white stone front stretching a good twelve feet from floor to ceiling. Embedded in the stone above the fireplace's dark opening was a hand-hewn cedar mantel, polished with care and age. Jack's heart swelled at the amount of time and skill that had gone into the overall design, but it quickly took a nosedive when his gaze hit on the gas space heater wedged in the firebox where logs should be resting, waiting for the flare of a match.

Leaving Alayna standing in the doorway, he crossed the room and knelt down before the hearth. He leaned over, bracing his hands on the uneven stone, and looked up, craning his neck so that he could see up the flue. Sure enough, weathered boards sealed off the chimney. He poked at the boards almost wistfully, thinking of the waste…and, too, of the disappointment he'd heard in Alayna's voice when she'd told him she was going to have to forego re-opening the fireplace in order to stay on budget. He straightened, dusting soot from his hands. "I can open her back up," he said, avoiding her gaze. "'Course I'll check out the chimney and flue to make sure that everything's in working order first. But I won't charge you any extra for my time."

"Oh, no!" she cried, hurrying across the room. "I can't allow you to do the work for free."

Jack frowned as he looked down at her, seeing nothing but a deep, blue pool of compassion in her eyes. The idea that she would think of his needs, and not her own, baffled him. In his opinion, and based on his personal experience, the gentler sex was, as a rule, selfish and demanding. Was this woman real? he asked himself. When he felt himself being sucked deeper and deeper into her gaze, drawn by the compassion he saw in her eyes, he backed away from her.

"Not much work involved," he insisted briskly.

"Somebody along the line probably just got tired of cutting wood and sealed off the fireplace, choosing instead to use gas to heat the room." He gave an impatient gesture with his hand. "Let's see the rest of it."

Thankfully she let the subject drop. With nothing but a curious glance in his direction, she led the way to the stairway.

"The master bedroom is downstairs," she explained over her shoulder, "but Frank finished all the remodeling there before he left. You'll need to focus on the rooms upstairs." The soles of her sandals scraped lightly on the oak-planked stairs as she climbed higher, drawing Jack's gaze to her feet.

He stood at the bottom step, his eyes sliding up over her ankles and to the gentle curve of her calf. A warmth crawled up his neck and down to his groin as her elevated position on the stairway above him revealed more and more of her bare legs to him.

And he silently prayed she was wearing panties.

He wasn't sure what he'd do if he discovered she wasn't. It had been a long time since he'd been with a woman in the biblical sense, and he didn't know if he had the willpower needed to resist the sight of so much tempting flesh. He swallowed hard, paralyzed as much by the feelings of lust building as he was by the sight before him. He tried to remember the last woman who had stirred thoughts like these, but quickly gave up. It had been way too long.

"Upstairs," she said, lifting a hand from the rail to gesture above her, "are four more bedrooms." On the landing, she turned to look back at Jack and stopped when she saw that he was still standing in the hallway below. "Are you coming?"

"Yeah," he said, his voice husky, staring at her and

trying his damnedest not to think about those panties. The idea that he'd even think about a woman's panties was a relatively new one, and a definite improvement over his thoughts for the last several months. This woman was pushing buttons and getting a response to hankerings he was sure he'd lost long ago.

Could this be the end of his wanderings?

He cleared his throat, and started up the stairs. "Yeah," he said with more enthusiasm, thinking he might have just landed himself in heaven—or hell, depending on how the situation turned out. "I'm right behind you."

Alayna waited until he'd caught up with her, then opened a door on her left. "I don't plan to do anything too major in here," she explained. "Just freshen things up a bit. Paint. Drapes. Maybe add shelving for toys and such."

Jack's head snapped around at the mention of toys. "You have kids?"

At the question, the smile that seemed her constant companion melted right off her face. She glanced away from him and to the far window with its view of the pond. "No," she replied with what almost sounded like embarrassment. Then she forced her chin up and a confident smile to her lips as she turned her gaze back to his. "At least, none of my own."

Jack felt the blood drain right out of him at the hope he saw in her eyes. And just when he was beginning to feel a little interest, a little heat in the old furnace, she had to go and mention kids. A damn shame, too, he thought sadly, admiring the sway of her hips as she walked away from him and across the room. She was a beautiful woman. Sexy. Friendly.

And convenient.

He shook his head and folded his arms across his chest. But he wasn't getting involved with a woman who wanted kids. Not Jack Cordell. No how, no way.

Two

While Jack was bemoaning his bad luck with women, a
horn blasted outside and Alayna hurried to the window
and peered down below. One look and she cried, "Oh,
no!" then whirled and ran past him.

Wondering what she'd seen that had put that horrified
look on her face, Jack crossed to the window and looked
down. A yellow school bus was parked out front, its cau-
tion lights blinking.

Jack's stomach clenched at the sight of the small faces
pressed against the windows.

As he watched, unable to move, the bus's doors folded
back and a book bag came sailing through the door. A
small boy appeared next, one shoulder hunched up defensively against the bus driver who was shoving him
down the steps in front of him.

Every muscle in Jack's body tensed, poised for flight.
He had to get out of there.

But before he could make good his escape, Alayna appeared on the front lawn below him, the skirt of her baggy dress whipping around her legs as she raced toward the bus. Jack shifted his gaze back to the little boy. He couldn't hear what the bus driver was saying to the kid, and didn't want to hear. He wanted out in the worst sort of way. Out of this house. Out of this town.

He just plain wanted out.

You have my word. I'll see the job done.

Jack groaned, leaning to plant his hands against the window's sill and his forehead against its glass as his words came back to haunt him. He squeezed his eyes shut. He'd given his word. And Jack Cordell never backed down once he'd given his word.

He opened his eyes with a frustrated sigh and saw that a little girl had joined the trio on the drive. She was standing off to the side, her chin dipped to her chest, a threadbare-one-eyed teddy bear hugged tight to her chest, her thumb sunk deeply into her mouth. The boy was kicking and swinging at the driver, and Alayna was trying her best to wedge herself between the two.

When the bus driver gave Alayna a shove, roughly knocking her out of his way, Jack straightened, curling his hands into tight fists. Whether he wanted to be in this house, or not, was no longer important. He couldn't stand by and watch a man rough up a woman.

He stormed from the room, down the stairs and out onto the lawn. Alayna was already back on her feet and was preparing to jump back in the fray.

"Let the kid go."

The order was delivered with just enough volume and with enough punch behind it to make the boy quit his thrashing, the bus driver to quit his shouting and the little girl to drop her thumb from her mouth. All four—Alayna included—turned to stare at Jack, slack-jawed.

Jack moved closer. "I said, let the kid go."

The bus driver squared his shoulders. "And who do you think you are, telling me what to do?"

"*Who* I am isn't important. What I'm telling you *is*. Let the kid go."

"He cussed me."

"I *said*, let the boy go."

The bus driver eyed Jack a moment as if measuring his chances if it came to a fight, then scowled. He gave the boy a shove, knocking him up against Jack's leg. The boy fell to his knees but immediately scrambled back to his feet, curling his hands into fists. Jack put a hand on the boy's shoulder, firmly holding him in place.

With a sneer at the kid, the driver turned on Alayna. "I'm telling you for the last time," he said, shaking a threatening finger in her face. "That smart-mouthed kid ain't ridin' my bus no more. I don't have to put up with that kind of sass, 'specially not from a snot-nosed, motherless brat." With that, he wheeled around and stomped back up the steps of his bus. The door snapped back into place, then, with a grinding of gears, the bus pulled away.

Jack tightened his hand on the boy's shoulder and spun him around to face him. "Did you cuss him?"

The kid glared up at Jack, meeting his gaze belligerently. "Yeah. I called him an old fart, 'cause he is one."

"Go to your room." Jack wasn't sure where the order came from, or even why he was involving himself in a situation that was definitely none of his business. But he had, and though he'd come to the kid's defense, he knew the boy was in the wrong and needed a good reprimanding.

The boy swelled up as if he wanted to argue Jack's

right to tell him what to do, but Alayna quickly inter-
vened. "Go on upstairs, Billy, and put your school things
away. And take Molly with you. I'll be up in a minute."

Though Jack could tell the boy didn't want to obey
the order, to his credit, he followed Alayna's instructions.
"Come on, Molly," he muttered, stooping to scrape his
book bag from the ground. "Something stinks out here,"
he added, shooting a dark look Jack's way.

Molly sidestepped her way past Jack, her eyes wide
and watchful as she stared up at him. When she'd made
it safely past him, she tucked her teddy bear tighter
against her chest and ran to catch up with Billy. On the
porch, she bent and scooped up the cat, then, with a last
nervous glance at Jack, she slipped inside the door.

Alayna watched her charges disappear into the house.
"I'm sorry," she said, then turned to look at Jack. She
sighed when she saw his disapproving scowl. "I'm afraid
my children didn't make a very good first impression,
did they?"

One thick eyebrow shot up in surprise. "Those two are
your kids?"

"Technically, no. They are my foster children."

His scowl returned.

Alayna wrinkled her nose as she continued to peer up
at him. "I guess you don't care for children any more
than you care for cats, huh?"

"Not particularly. And that boy there," he said with
a jerk of his chin toward the house, "needs to have the
seat of his pants warmed. He's got a mouth on him."

Alayna nodded her agreement, though already dreading the confrontation. "Yes. I'll talk to Billy."

Jack grunted, indicating his doubt on the effectiveness
of having a talk with a kid like Billy.

"You haven't changed your mind, have you?" Alayna asked uncertainly. "You'll stay and do the remodeling?"

Jack glanced toward his truck, the temptation to climb back in it and drive away so strong he had to brace his knees to keep from giving in to it. "I gave my word," he said, setting his jaw. "I'll see the job done."

Jack awakened early, as was his habit, to find the sky beyond his window washed with the pinks and lavenders signifying dawn's arrival. The bed he slept on was an old one, but comfortable, and a definite improvement over the bedroll he'd been sleeping on for the last couple of months, spread out over the bed of his truck. He rolled to his side, tucking an arm beneath his head, and stared out the window, praying that the events of the day before had never happened, that he'd wake up any minute and realize it was all a bad dream.

But he wasn't asleep, and this was no bad dream that he'd wake from. The view of the Pond House through the cabin's window was proof enough of that.

The Pond House. A fitting—if simplistic—name for the house, since the structure had been built beside a pond. Yet, the name was a poetic one, too, reflective of the setting and the natural materials that had been used in its construction. White limestone, rough cedar, combined with a lot of glass to take advantage of the views. It was a beautiful place, well constructed, though still in need of repair. There was a peacefulness about the place and its setting that seemed to tug at him.

Peaceful. That word again. He frowned, thinking how the day before he'd thought the same thing about the town of Driftwood when he'd been staring at its main street through the café's window. Now here he was planted right smack-dab in the middle of it all—the town, the house, the pastoral setting—and he sure as hell didn't feel very peaceful. Not when he considered the kids who inhabited the house…or the woman who cared for them.

He glanced at the bedside table and at the bottle of whiskey sitting on top of it. His friend. His companion. His catharsis for a pain that just wouldn't go away.

He frowned and reached for the bottle, curling his fingers around its neck. Amber liquid sloshed against its side as he leaned over and shoved the bottle underneath the bed and out of his sight. The whiskey had failed to work its magical charm for him this time. His dreams during the night, though different from his past ones, were no less disturbing. They had been filled with an angel-faced woman with eyes so deep a blue a man could drown in them, and a gentle touch that made his skin heat and his heart yearn for things that could never be.

With a groan, he rolled to his side again, and stared out the window. As if his thoughts had drawn her, the back door of the Pond House opened and the woman who had filled his dreams stepped out onto the flagstone patio.

Alayna.

She wore a long, cotton robe, the same shade of blue as her eyes. It billowed around her legs in the early-morning breeze like a cloud in a summer sky. Barefoot and with her blond hair still mussed with sleep, she looked young and innocent…and good enough to eat. While he watched, she hugged her arms up under her breasts, tipped her face up to the sky and drew in a deep, cleansing breath. A soft, sensual smile curved her lips as she filled her lungs with the fresh, early-morning air. Even from his distance, Jack could see the rise of her breasts over her folded arms, and his groin tightened in response.

Damn, but she was pretty, and as sexy as any woman

he'd ever seen. He shifted, easing the unexpected ache that jumped to life between his legs. Unable to look away from her, he continued to watch as she walked around the patio, pausing to fluff a floral pillow on a chair, then stooping to pull a weed from a terra-cotta pot filled with pink geraniums and trailing ivy. With her movements, the robe parted, revealing a brief peek at tanned legs, and when she stooped, the top gaped, baring an even more enticing view of the valley between her breasts.

Eve couldn't have waved that apple under Adam's nose with a greater effect.

Jack felt the desire mounting and rolled to his back and away from the tempting sight, his eyes wide, his breath coming fast and hard. He fisted his hands in the tangle of bed linens, forced his gaze to remain on the ceiling and made himself draw in three deep breaths.

Kids, he reminded himself. The woman had kids. And Jack Cordell wanted no part of them. The woman *or* her brood.

Alayna stuck her head out the kitchen door and offered Jack a sunny smile. "Good morning! You're up early."

Seeing that she still wore the same blue robe he'd seen her in earlier, Jack frowned and glanced away, setting his toolbox on the flagstone patio. "Didn't see any sense in wasting time getting started."

"Have you had breakfast?" She laughed before he could answer, flapping a dismissing hand at him. "Of course you haven't," she said, shaking her head at the foolishness of her question. "You wouldn't have had a chance to stock the cabin with food, yet." She waved her hand again, this time gesturing for him to come inside. "I was just whipping up a batch of pancakes. There's plenty for two."

Without waiting for an answer, she slipped back into the kitchen, letting the door close softly behind her.

Jack stared through the mesh screen at the shadowed form moving beyond it, his empty stomach warring with good sense, his mind worrying with the fear of facing those kids again. In the end, his stomach won out.

His feet heavy with dread, he opened the door and stepped inside. The smell of coffee greeted him first, followed quickly by the scent of bacon frying. Then his gaze rested on Alayna, standing before the stove, looking much the same as she had earlier that morning when he'd seen her on the patio—her feet still bare, her hair still tousled from sleep.

He glanced around uneasily. "Where are the kids?"

"Oh, they've already left for school." She glanced over her shoulder, but missed the relaxing of his shoulders, though she must have seen the question in his eyes. "My cousin's son drove them," she explained, then turned back to the griddle with a sigh. "Yesterday wasn't the first time we've had a problem on the bus…and I'm sure it won't be the last. Molly says that Mr. Evert, the bus driver, picks on Billy."

Jack grunted his doubt and won a slight frown from Alayna.

"I know that what Billy did was wrong," she said as she turned back to the stove. "But he's just a little boy and he's having a difficult time adjusting to all the changes in his life. Mr. Evert's an adult. Surely he could be a little more understanding, a little more compassionate."

"The boy needs to learn to control his mouth and show respect for his elders."

Alayna sighed again, and poured batter on the griddle. "Yes. You're right, of course. Still…" She gave her head a shake, then turned slightly, offering Jack a grateful smile. "I appreciated your help yesterday. Having a male influence around will be a help to Billy, I'm sure."

Jack intended to set her straight real quick about his willingness to get involved in the kids' lives, but her movement caused her robe to gape a bit, revealing the swell of a breast, the shadowed cleavage that lay between. The sight burned away all rational thought. He ripped off his cap and gripped it by its bill, needing to fill his hands with something other than tempting flesh. "Is there something I can do to help?" he asked, forcing his gaze away from her and to the clock on the wall.

"You can set the table, if you like. The plates are in the cupboard—" she gave her head a nod in that direction "—and the silver is in the first drawer to the left."

Jack tossed his cap to the counter, crossed to the sink and began to wash his hands.

"You know," she said thoughtfully as she turned thick strips of bacon in an iron skillet, "it's really foolish for you to even consider stocking up on a lot of groceries. Cooking for one is difficult, I know, and awfully lonely." She tossed a sympathetic smile in Jack's direction. "Why don't you just plan to eat your meals here with us?"

Jack's fingers slipped on the bar of soap and it shot out of his hands, smacking against the side of the chipped porcelain sink with a loud *thunk*. He swallowed hard, trying to think up an excuse to decline. "I wouldn't want to put you to the trouble," he mumbled and stuck his hands beneath the water, wishing he could stick his head beneath the cool spray, as well.

"Oh, no bother." She graced him with yet another smile.

Without answering, Jack tore off a strip of paper towels and dried his hands, already regretting accepting her invitation for breakfast and wondering how he was going to wiggle his way out of sharing meals with her and her brood. He reached for the plates, then opened the drawer she'd indicated and stacked the necessary utensils on top. Crossing to the table, he arranged place settings on opposite sides of the table.

"There's coffee already made, or, if you'd prefer, there's orange juice in the refrigerator."

Hoping the caffeine would clear his head a little and settle his nerves, Jack mumbled, "Coffee's fine," and headed for the coffeemaker on the counter. By the time he'd poured himself a cup, Alayna was setting a platter of bacon and stacks of golden pancakes in the center of the table. She took a seat, gesturing for him to join her.

"Have you decided where you'd like to start work today?" she asked as she served first his plate, then hers.

Jack pulled a napkin across his lap, but kept his gaze fixed on his plate. He wasn't sure he trusted that robe of hers to stay in place, not with the way she was flapping those arms of hers around, and he didn't think he could handle another glimpse of those creamy breasts. He had to get out of this place, he told himself, and the sooner the better. "You never said what all you wanted done."

Alayna poured syrup over her pancakes. "Frank took care of the major repairs before he left, but there are still quite a few things that need attention. There are two baths upstairs. The shower leaks like a sieve in one of them, though both could stand some remodeling. And there are a few changes I'd like made in the bedrooms." She waved her fork vaguely. "Enlarging closets. Adding shelving. Painting. That kind of thing." She parted her lips and slipped a forkful of pancakes between them. She smiled at Jack as she chewed. "But I think what I'd like to do first is tackle the wall in the breakfast nook. You really *aroused* my curiosity with your comments about the wood hidden beneath the wallpaper.''

The emphasis she placed on the word ''aroused'' had Jack snapping his gaze to hers. He immediately regretted the action. Her face was flushed with excitement, her blue eyes bright with expectancy. The craziest notion bubbled up out of nowhere…he wanted to lean across the table and cover her mouth with his, and show her what it meant to be *really* aroused.

Slowly he dragged his napkin from his lap and wiped it across his mouth, then across the perspiration beading his forehead before wadding it in a ball against his thigh. ''Then that's where I'll start,'' he said, picking up his fork.

''What will we need to do?''

Jack jerked his head up again. ''We?'' he repeated, his face going slack. ''*You're* planning on helping me?''

She laid down her fork, her shoulders drooping right along with her expression. ''Well, yes,'' she said uncertainly. ''But I won't get in your way,'' she added quickly, ''if that's what you're worried about. I just thought the work would go that much faster if I helped.''

Jack set aside his own fork, his appetite suddenly gone. The idea of working alongside Alayna and the forced intimacy involved had created another, more dangerous hunger.

Paper hung in tattered strips, already revealing sections of tongue-and-groove boards by the time Alayna returned to the breakfast room. Thankfully she had exchanged her robe for a pair of baggy cotton slacks and a man's tailored white shirt. Even though she was now covered from neck to toe, somehow she still managed to look sexy, a fact that irritated Jack.

Out of the corner of his eye, he watched her roll up her sleeves and knew he was going to have to think of some way to dissuade her from helping him. He wasn't sure his system could take much more temptation.

"Okay, so what do you want me to do?" she asked, her voice full of enthusiasm.

Keeping his eyes focused on his work, Jack tipped his head toward the soggy wallpaper he'd already ripped from the wall and dropped to the floor. "You can pick up the scrap paper and put it in the garbage sack I've set out."

"That's all?"

Jack bit back a smile of satisfaction at the disappointment he heard in her voice. Realizing that this might be just the way to get rid of her, he kept his gaze on the wall in front of him. "Well, I suppose you could start on the plumbing in the bath upstairs, if you'd rather do something that requires more skill."

"But I don't know anything about plumbing."

Jack dropped his hand to his side, and slowly turned to look at her, his posture that of a man at the end of his patience. "Well, then why don't you pick up the paper, like I suggested?"

To his surprise—and disappointment—Alayna dropped to her knees and began to scrape the soiled and gum-slickened paper into a pile.

"What do we do after all the paper is off?"

Jack stared down at her, watching in growing amazement as she crawled around on the drop cloth he'd spread on the floor, picking up the soggy paper and stuffing it into the garbage bag. She didn't flinch, didn't curl her nose, didn't argue. Hell, she didn't even complain! She just did as he'd instructed. A woman of obvious breeding, and a doctor, no less, willing to lower herself to perform-

ing menial labor? The woman was an oddity. A paradox.
A total opposite to his ex-wife who had thought herself
too good to get her hands dirty. He gave his head a shake,
clearing it of the old memories, and went back to tearing
off paper.

"Once the paper's off," he said, firming his voice as
he refocused on her question, "we'll have to clean the
wall, removing all the old paste and any residue the paper
left. Then we'll give it a good rubbing with a mixture of
linseed oil and a little turpentine. If you're satisfied with
the look, then we'll brush on a clear sealer. If not, we
might want to first add a stain, then the sealer."

At his use of the word "we," Alayna sat up and
rocked back on her heels, wiping her palms down her
thighs. "You'll let me help you do all those things?"

Jack angled his head to look at her and saw the almost
childlike hopefulness in her eyes. Quickly he looked
away, refusing to be moved by it. "We'll see."

Alayna dropped back down to her knees and started
picking up the paper faster. "Neat. I love to paint." At
Jack's doubtful grunt, she scooped up a pile of paper and
stuffed it into the bag. "I really do," she insisted. "When
I opened my first office in Raleigh, I was operating on a
shoestring. It was a dump. Really depressing. I completely redecorated it and I did all the painting myself. I
even did a mural of a jungle with all these wild animals
peeking out from behind the trees and plants."

Jack turned to look at her. *A mural of a jungle?* What
was she, a veterinarian? "What kind of doctor are you,
anyway?"

"A child psychologist."

Jack's stomach plunged to his feet. He quickly turned
away and picked up the brush and put it in motion.

Intent on gathering up the paper, Alayna went on with

her explanation, unaware of his reaction to her choice in careers. "I specialized in cases of abuse and neglect. My clients were usually sent to me by the courts." Having picked up all the paper he'd discarded, she rocked back on her heels and watched while he brushed water over another section of the wall. "My husband thought I was crazy." She chuckled, remembering. "He hated painting with a passion."

She slowly sobered as other memories of her ex-husband slipped into her mind, and she dropped her gaze to her hand, unconsciously rubbing at the spot where she'd once worn his ring. "In fact, he hated my office, my career, my clients. He couldn't stand imperfection in any form." A shiver chased down her spine at the unwanted reminder, and she straightened, lifting her gaze to Jack...and found him staring at her.

"You're married?"

At the stunned look on his face, she quickly shook her head. "No. Divorced." When he continued to stare at her, she returned the question. "Are *you* married?"

"No." He turned back to the wall, and peeled a strip of paper from it, letting it fall to the drop cloth, then added, "Divorced."

She stared at his back, wondering if the sadness, the emptiness she'd seen in his eyes was a result of the divorce. "Were you married long?"

"Long enough." Jack ripped another strip of paper from the wall and dropped it to the floor and, along with it, it seemed, the topic of discussion. "There's a scraper in my toolbox. Get it for me."

Alayna saw the tenseness in his shoulders, heard it in his clipped order. Avoidance. She knew the symptoms well. And knew, too, how unhealthy the tactic was.

She crossed to his toolbox, found the scraper he'd requested, then returned, holding it out to him as she studied his profile. "Divorce can be painful," she offered quietly, hoping to draw him back into the conversation. But he didn't bite. The only sign that he'd heard her was an increased tenseness in his jaw. His gaze remained fixed on the wall.

"Was yours a painful divorce?" she asked, angling her head to better see his face, his expression.

Jack flung the paper he'd just torn from the wall to the floor and bent to pick up the paintbrush again. His lips remained stubbornly pressed together as he swiped water over a new section of faded wallpaper with angry strokes.

His refusal to talk about his divorce told Alayna what he refused to admit. His divorce *had* been painful. From experience, she knew that talking helped. "Jack?" she prodded gently. "Was it painful?"

He tossed his paintbrush back into the can, then looked at her over his shoulder. "Don't try crawling around in my head, Doc. You might not like what you find."

Alayna refused to let him intimidate her. "Sounds as if you've had experience with a psychologist. Judging by your tone, it wasn't a very happy one. Is that true?"

"Bingo," he muttered bitterly and picked up his paintbrush again. "Paid a damn fortune to spill my guts to some tight-assed, sanctimonious stranger who sat in a chair and mumbled 'hmm' all the time. When that didn't work, I paid another wad of money in attorney fees." Slowly he turned to look at Alayna, his mouth thinned in a grim, thin line. "Now there's somebody you might enjoy psychoanalyzing, Doc. My ex's divorce lawyer. Smiled the whole time he was ripping out my heart and draining the blood right out of me. I'll bet you'd get a kick out of digging around in his gray matter."

Unaffected by his bitter tone, Alayna listened, enthralled. Jack was talking. This was good.

"Cats, children, divorce lawyers." She ticked off each on her fingers, as if making a list, then glanced up at him, teasing him with a smile. "Is there anything or anyone else I should add to your list of dislikes?"

His scowled deepened. "Yeah. Angel-faced psychologists. They really get under my skin." He picked up the scraper and tossed it to her. She caught it deftly in one hand. "Now, are you going to yap your jaws all day, or are you going to work?"

"Oddly enough," she replied, unoffended, "I can talk and work at the same time. Can you?"

"Yeah," he replied irritably, "if the topic's interesting." He stooped to pick up his paintbrush again, then turned his back to her. "Unfortunately, this particular one bores me stiff."

Three

"**M**audie tells me that you've hired a new remodeler."

Alayna handed Mandy a glass of iced tea, then shuddered visibly as she sank onto a patio chair opposite her cousin. "Yes, and I can just imagine what all Maudie had to say on *that* subject."

"Oh, let's see," Mandy replied, tapping a finger against her chin, as if trying to recall the details of the conversation. "Something about Frank scamming you out of thousands of dollars, and what a softhearted little fool you are. Then I believe she mentioned something about this man you hired to replace Frank being a good-looking hunk, and that she is sure you hired him just to satisfy this insatiable need of yours for wild sex and—"

Alayna snorted. "Oh, yeah," she said sarcastically, "that was it, all right."

"*—and,*" Mandy continued pointedly, trying hard not to smile, "this same man—the one, by the way, who was hired strictly for his sexual prowess—will also steal you blind, the same as Frank did.'' She lifted her glass of tea, and smiled at Alayna from behind it. ''I think that's about all she had to say on the subject.''

Alayna arched a brow. ''Are you sure?'' she asked dryly.

Mandy tossed back her head and laughed. ''No. But those are the best parts.''

Annoyed, Alayna folded her arms beneath her breasts and crossed her legs, her foot pumping like an oil derrick. ''I swear. I love Maudie to death, but there are times...''

''I know, I know,'' Mandy agreed, still laughing. ''But she means well.''

In spite of her annoyance, Alayna found herself chuckling, too, as she thought of Maudie with her mother-hen-heart and her bossy ways. ''Yes. It's her only redeeming quality.''

Mandy nodded her agreement, then glanced around. ''Where is he, anyway? I thought for sure I would be interrupting something really sordid by dropping by without calling first.''

''He went to town to pick up some supplies.''

''Oh, well. Maybe next time.'' As she sipped her tea, Mandy continued to look around, making note of the changes since her last visit. ''You've really done a lot with the place.''

Alayna followed her cousin's gaze, smiling her pleasure at all she'd managed to accomplish. Frank had completed a lot of the work before he'd run out on her, and after only a week, Jack had done quite a bit more. ''Yes, but there's still a lot to be done.''

''All in due time.''

Alayna's brow creased with worry. ''But that's just it. I don't know how much time I have. I want to be ready if they should call and have more children needing a home.''

Mandy leaned over and gave Alayna's knee a comforting pat. "You'll be ready." She smiled at the doubt she saw in Alayna's eyes. "Have I told you that I'm proud of you?"

Alayna blushed, uncomfortable with the praise. "About a thousand times."

Mandy settled back in her chair. "Well, I can't say it enough. Few women would consider doing what you are doing, and fewer still would be able to do it well."

Alayna scooted to the edge of her chair, reaching out to clasp her cousin's hand in hers. "Oh, Mandy," she said her voice filled with doubt. "I want to do this well, I really do, but I'm frightened. Billy and Molly seem to be doing well enough, but what if I somehow fail these children and do them more harm than good?"

Mandy set aside her tea glass and leaned forward, taking both of Alayna's hands in hers and squeezing. "You won't let them down. You have years of experience dealing with troubled children, and the sincere desire to help them. That's all that's truly required. That and a whole lot of love, which you seem to have in abundance."

With emotion clogging her throat, Alayna gave Mandy's hands a grateful squeeze. "Thanks, cuz. After the run-in I had with the bus driver and my inability to persuade him or the district's transportation department to rescind his decision, I needed to hear that."

"Don't worry about that old cranky bus driver. Jaime doesn't mind driving the kids to school." Impulsively Mandy leaned and pecked a kiss on Alayna's cheek, then pressed a fingertip to the spot as she leaned back to meet her cousin's gaze. "We're glad you're here," she said softly. "All of us. And we're glad that you've decided to make the Pond House and the Double-Cross Heart Ranch your home.''

Alayna looked around, her fingers still clasped tightly around Mandy's. ''It feels like home,'' she said, and at that moment realized the truth in the statement. She cut her gaze back to Mandy's and grinned. ''Do you remember when we were younger, and Daddy would bring us here for visits in the summer, and we'd have those wonderful sleepovers, with all the cousins camped out in one room?''

Mandy sighed wistfully, releasing Alayna's hand to settle back in her chair. ''Oh, we had some good times, didn't we? Sam was always thinking up daredevil things for us to do. Remember the time we put baby oil and flour in Merideth's hair while she was sleeping?''

Alayna laughed, the sound rich and full in the quiet afternoon. ''Do I ever! Merideth was furious. She always hated getting her hair or her clothes messed up.''

Mandy chuckled. ''And she hasn't changed a bit. She's still as persnickety as ever about her appearance. Just the other day—''

''Excuse me.''

Alayna and Mandy both jumped at the unexpected intrusion.

Alayna's breath came out in a rush when she saw Jack standing at the edge of the patio. ''Oh, my stars, Jack,'' she cried, laughing weakly. ''You nearly scared the life out of me.''

Jack cut a glance from Alayna to the woman sitting beside her, then back. ''Sorry. I brought the paint samples to show you, but they can wait.'' He turned to go, but Alayna called out to him, stopping him.

''Jack! Wait!'' When he turned, she rose, and Mandy stood as well. Wrapping an arm at her cousin's waist,

Alayna drew Mandy with her as she crossed to him. "I want you to meet my cousin, Mandy McCloud Barrister. Mandy, this is Jack Cordell."

Mandy extended her hand in greeting, a smile much like Alayna's warming her eyes as she peered up at him. "Hi, Jack. I've heard a lot about you." She gave Alayna an arched look, one that Jack didn't understand, then returned her gaze to his, adding, "And I have to say that you are *all* Maudie described and more."

Remembering the sharp-tongued waitress from the café and her comments about his predecessor Frank, Jack frowned, not at all sure what the woman might have said about him. "Pleased to meet you," he mumbled uneasily.

Mandy's smile widened as if at some private joke. "The pleasure is all mine, I assure you." She withdrew her hand and turned to Alayna. "Well, I guess I better get back to the house. Jesse and Jaime will be coming home soon and wanting their dinner." Her eyes brightened. "Why don't y'all have dinner with us? We'd love to have you." She looked at Jack, including him in the invitation. "I know that my husband and son will want to meet you and welcome you to the Double-Cross. How about it?"

Alayna saw the look of alarm slowly spreading across Jack's face, the way his fingers convulsed on the paint samples he still held. But to her way of thinking an evening in the company of a happily married couple might be just what Jack needed, since his own experience in matrimony seemed to have left nothing but negative memories. "Thanks, Mandy," she replied before Jack could respond, "we'd love to."

Jack whipped his head around to frown at her. "You and the kids can go. I'm not much on socializing." He gave his head a quick bob in Mandy's direction. "If you'll excuse me, I've got work to do."

Alayna's heart sank as she watched him stalk away.

"Was it something I said?" Mandy asked uncertainly.

Alayna forced a smile and slung an arm around her cousin's shoulder as she walked with her to her truck. "No. It's Jack. He is—well, I don't know what he is exactly. Sad. Bitter." She stopped at the side of her cousin's truck and gave Mandy a squeeze before withdrawing her arm. "But mainly just stubborn."

"Is he dangerous?"

Alayna started to laugh, but quickly swallowed it when she saw the seriousness in Mandy's expression. "No," she said, shaking her head, instinctively knowing somehow that her claim was true. "He's not dangerous." She glanced toward the barn and watched as Jack heaved a stack of two-by-fours over the side of his truck. The muscles in his arms bulged with the effort. "Angry," she said, recognizing the signs, but unsure of their source. "Mad at the world," she added, noting his dark expression. She looked back at Mandy and smiled reassuringly. "But not dangerous."

"You'll still bring the kids over for dinner, won't you?"

"Of course I will," Alayna assured her. "What time do you want us?"

Jack grabbed another stack of two-by-fours, muscles straining, and tossed them over the side of his truck. Bracing his hands at his hips, he hauled in a deep breath, then slowly blew it out. He glanced toward the drive in time to see Mandy leave.

A son, she'd said. She'd wanted him to have dinner with her husband and her son. Bringing a shaky hand to his forehead, he swiped at the sweat that had popped out on his forehead. Sharing meals with Alayna and her brood of kids was unnerving enough, but the thought of sharing a dinner with a family was worse.

In fact, it sounded a whole lot like hell to Jack.

Dusk had settled over the countryside by the time Alayna returned home from her cousin's and tucked the children into bed for the night. After picking up their clothes from the bathroom floor where they'd left them, she slipped into Molly's room, deciding to check on her little charges one more time before heading downstairs for the night.

She smiled down at the sleeping Molly, then drew the sheet a little closer to the child's chin. Molly sighed in her sleep and hugged the ragged teddy bear she slept with closer to her chest. The teddy bear was all that Molly had arrived with when she'd been delivered to Alayna. That and the clothes on her back.

Molly's story was a sad, if familiar one. Her mother, a drug addict, left her alone for days at a time, with no food, no one to look after her, while she chased the next fix, or the man who could buy it for her. Repeated complaints from neighbors in the apartment complex where Molly and her mother had lived had resulted in the child being taken away from her mother.

And now she was in Alayna's care.

Though physically the child didn't appear to have suffered from her mother's neglect, the emotional scars were there. The child never smiled, rarely spoke and she never let the ragged teddy bear out of her sight or reach.

Smiling wistfully, Alayna smoothed the child's hair from her forehead and placed a light kiss there. Two weeks. Two weeks she'd had Molly with her, and she had already fallen hopelessly in love. She drew a fingertip lightly down the length of the child's freckled nose, wondering why God would see fit to bless Molly's mother with a child, a woman who obviously didn't want the burden, and not herself, who would gladly sacrifice anything for the opportunity to give birth to a baby.

She straightened, shoving the bitter thought aside. She had children, she reminded herself. Two already, and the promise of more to come.

With that positive thought, she crossed the hall to Billy's room.

As usual, she found him sprawled on his stomach and the bed covers tangled at the foot of the bed. An action figure lay beneath his lax fingers. Billy never just went to bed and to sleep, as other children did. He fought sleep as if it were an enemy that would capture him and never let him go. Though Alayna insisted on a strict bedtime schedule, Billy always took a toy to bed with him, a compromise they'd arrived at together. He'd play with the toy until he collapsed from sheer exhaustion.

Alayna knew less about Billy's history than she did about Molly's, and she wondered what events in his life caused him to fear sleep so much. He avoided any questions she asked, and was a master at changing the subject to a less invasive one. She knew that he'd been in another foster home before being assigned to her, but all she'd been told was that the prior situation simply hadn't worked out.

With a regretful shake of her head, she withdrew the toy from beneath his small hand, placed it on the shelf Jack had built on the wall beside the bed, then pulled the sheet up and over him, tucking it around his slender shoulders. In time, she told herself, she'd discover his secrets, what nightmares had shaped his life, and she would help him deal with them.

She leaned over and pressed a kiss to his forehead, just as she had to Molly's, knowing full well he'd never accept the affectionate display if awake. She tiptoed from his room, relieved to know that her little charges were settled peacefully for the night.

That just left Jack to deal with.

Pensively she started down the stairs. Although she'd enjoyed having dinner with Mandy's family, and watching Molly and Billy interact in a family setting, she hadn't been able to keep thoughts of Jack far from her mind. In her estimation, the look of alarm that had come into his eyes when Mandy had offered the dinner invitation signaled more than just an antisocial behavior. A whole lot more. And she was determined to find out what spawned the reaction.

At the kitchen door, she glanced in the direction of the cabin, intending to seek him out, but found the cabin dark. Certain that he wouldn't have gone to bed so early, she glanced toward the pond. In the gathering dusk, she saw him sitting on the edge of the weathered pier that jutted out over the water's mirrorlike surface. She stepped out onto the patio, closing the door softly behind her, then stopped and drew in a deep, shuddering breath, her gaze still fixed on his shadowed form.

He looked so lonely sitting there, staring out at the horizon...yet so unbelievably sexy. A dangerous combination to her way of thinking. He sat with one leg raised, an elbow hooked over his knee. His position placed a strain on the back of his black T-shirt, pulling the knit fabric taut across his back. Broad shoulders. Firm pads of muscle. She sighed as she traced the long, bumpy path of his spine with her gaze until it disappeared beneath the waist of his jeans. *Maudie was right,* she reflected lustfully. *He* is *a good-looking hunk.*

And she had about as much business thinking lusty thoughts as she did—well, she didn't have any business thinking such thoughts about Jack Cordell, or any man, for that matter. As a woman, she had nothing to offer Jack. But as a psychologist, she reminded herself, she could possibly help him exorcize the demons that had robbed him of his smile, and left him so bitter and withdrawn.

Knowing full well he probably wouldn't welcome the company, she headed for the pier.

"You missed a good dinner."

His shoulders tensed at the sound of her voice, but he didn't turn around. Nor did he respond. She frowned at his back, but refused to let his indifference warn her off. She started down the planked pier, feeling its slight roll beneath her feet. "I think you would've enjoyed meeting Mandy's husband, Jesse, and their son, Jaime."

He squinted his eyes, staring hard at the sliver of red sun that seemed to have snagged on the peak of the highest hill. "I'm not much on socializing."

She dropped down beside him, drawing up her legs and tucking the long hem of her dress behind them. "So you've said." She angled her head to peer at him. "Still, I think you'd enjoy meeting Jesse and Jaime. Molly and Billy really like them, and they don't accept people easily." When he offered nothing in return, she stifled a sigh of frustration and turned her gaze on the sunset, too.

The sky was streaked with color—vibrant reds, soft purples, seductive blues.

"Beautiful, isn't it?" she said softly, enchanted as always by the dramatic display. His noncommittal grunt won a frown from her—though she received little satisfaction in making the gesture since he stubbornly refused to look at her, or acknowledge her presence. Unwilling to let his indifference chase her away, she turned her attention back to the horizon. Silence stretched between them, broken only by the croaking of frogs along the bank and the musical call of cicadas from the tall clumps of grass growing around it. The sounds brought back a wealth of memories.

"When I was young," she said, smiling wistfully, "I used to spend my summers here on the Double-Cross. All of the McCloud cousins would gather on this very pier and wait for the sun to disappear behind the hills. It was quite a sight. So colorful. So dramatic. Yet, so sad."

"Sad?" he repeated, cocking his head to the side to frown at her.

She met his gaze and smiled, pleased that she'd at last managed to pull a response from him. "Yes, sad." She looked again at the distant hills, nodding her head in that direction. "The sunset signaled the end of the day and was a reminder that we were one day closer to having to say goodbye. That always made us sad." She wrapped her arms around her knees, hugging her legs to her chest, drifting for a moment in a pleasant sea of childhood memories. "We were separated by hundreds of miles and sometimes we saw each other only once a year, but we were very, very close." She turned her cheek to the top of her knees and looked over at him. "Do you have family?"

He squinted harder at the sunset, and a muscle flexed on his jaw. "Yeah."

"Well...?" she prodded. "A brother? A sister? Parents?"

His lips thinned perceptibly. "One of each. Except for the sister." He frowned, then reached down beside him and picked up a bottle his leg had hidden from her before. Tipping back his head, he took a long swig, his Adam's apple bobbing with each slow swallow.

Jack Daniel's Old Time Quality Tennessee Sour Mash Whiskey, the label read. Alayna noted the level of liquid when he set the bottle down on the pier. Less than half full. "Are you drunk?" she asked, peering at him more closely.

He dragged the back of his wrist across his mouth. "Not yet."

"Are you *planning* on getting drunk?"

He turned his head to look at her, and she had to tighten her arms around her knees to keep from reaching out and smoothing away the deep lines of dissatisfaction that furrowed his forehead and puckered the corners of his mouth.

"Maybe." He lifted the bottle again, but this time he tipped it toward her. "Want to get drunk with me?"

By his measuring look, she knew that he was testing her, sure that she would decline. Just to spite him, she took the bottle, used the skirt of her dress to prudently wipe its lip clean, then took a dainty sip.

And choked.

Her eyes bugged wide, she fanned frantically at her face, her throat burning, her breath a ball of fire in her lungs.

Jack took the bottle of whiskey from her before she spilled it, and took a small sip. "Guess I'll be getting drunk alone," he said wryly. He cocked his head to look at her as he set the bottle aside, and she saw that one corner of his mouth was turned up slightly.

Alayna froze, her hand stopping in midwave, her mouth and eyes still gaped wide. He was smiling. Well, sort of smiling. And the smile did the most extraordinary things to his face. It softened his features, robbing him of that disgruntled look that he wore so well, and it put a gleam in his eyes, the life that had been missing before.

And his mouth. Still moist from the whiskey he'd drunk and reddened by the pressure of the bottle he'd pressed against them, his lips were full and inviting. All she could think about was pressing her own lips there and sipping at him, feeling the curve of his smile while absorbing his taste, his flavor, draining all the sadness and bitterness from inside him.

As she continued to stare, his smile widened, curving both sides of that sexy mouth. Then he was leaning toward her, his breath warm on her face. The sharp scent of whiskey filled her senses. Was he going to kiss her? she wondered, her heart skipping a beat at the thought. She shifted her gaze to his eyes at the same moment that his finger touched the bottom of her chin. He gently pushed up, and her teeth came together with a soft *click.*

"Careful," he warned, his voice husky. "You might catch a few flies."

"You smiled," she whispered, her disbelieving gaze locked on his. "I've never seen you smile before."

He lifted a shoulder. "Maybe because I haven't had anything to smile about." He shifted his weight to his hip, angling his body toward hers, trapping her raised knees in the curve created by his thighs and chest.

But his gaze never once left her face.

"You've got the most beautiful eyes," he whispered. He narrowed his own eyes, focusing on hers. "Blue. The deepest blue I believe I've ever seen. A man could drown in them."

Drugged by the huskiness in his voice, the intensity in his gaze, Alayna remained motionless, her praise-starved soul feeding on his every word.

He lifted his hand and brushed the tip of a finger almost reverently across her lower lashes. Her eyelids grew heavy at his touch, too heavy to hold up, while a delicious shiver chased down her spine. Then his finger was tracing her cheekbone, as light and teasing as a feather moving over her skin. "Soft," he murmured, his voice drawing nearer. The ball of his thumb moved to brush across her lower lip. "And oh, so sweet," he whispered. She felt his breath on her face, moist, hot, then his lips touched hers. Once. Twice. A brand searing her flesh.

She had time to draw in only one ragged breath before his mouth was closing fully over hers, capturing her lips, taking, feeding. His body forged closer, his chest a wall of heat and muscle against her arm. Lost to the sensation of his lips moving on hers, his texture, his taste, she was only vaguely aware of him shifting again. Then his hand was cupping her neck, the pad of his callused thumb stroking the long column of her throat. Her lips parted on a moan at the sensual play of flesh against flesh.

His thumb moved lower. Lower still. Until it nestled in the valley between her breasts. Her breath burned in her lungs as she waited for more of his touch, ached for him to take her fully in his hand.

Slowly he fanned his fingers, capturing her breast and gently kneading. Desire rose within her, a giant wave of need that threatened to drown her.

And she swallowed a moan of utter despair.

She was no good at this, she told herself. She was, at best, half a woman. Cold. Sexless. Hadn't her ex-husband told her that often enough? She had all the parts, technically knew the motions, but lacked the ability to put all those things together in a way that would pleasure a man. Another shiver shuddered its way through her—this one fed by panic.

She couldn't bear failing again. Not when she'd worked so hard to regain her confidence. Not when she was on the verge of realizing her dreams. She had to remain strong, in control, so that she could help the children. The two that were already with her, and those still to come.

On a sob, she tore her mouth from his, turning her face away. "No. Please," she begged, strangled by the tears that clogged her throat. "Don't."

Slowly Jack withdrew, his blood pumping wildly through his veins, need a deep, piercing ache in his groin, in his chest. He stared at Alayna's bent head, at the way she held one shoulder to her ear as if to ward off a blow. The desperation in her plea slowly registered and ripped a new wound through his already tattered heart.

No. Please. Don't.

He swallowed hard as her words echoed around him. Shame washed through him and he drew further away. He opened his hand and looked down at his palm, still feeling the warmth, the softness of her breast. What had come over him? What had possessed him to make a move like that? He closed his hand into a fist, his lips thinning. He didn't want to get involved with her. Even less, to hurt her. She was an angel. A woman who deserved a man who was willing to give her the children that she wanted so desperately.

"I'm sorry," he mumbled. "I—" But he couldn't think of an explanation for his actions—nothing but the truth, which was that he wanted her. Needed her. He yearned for her softness, her compassion, for just a slice of the joy and happiness in simply being alive that seemed to radiate from her every moment of every day.

But what did he have to give her in return? Nothing. Not one blame thing.

Snatching up the bottle of whiskey, Jack pushed himself to his feet. He strode down the pier, the weathered planks pitching beneath his feet as he all but ran from her. From temptation.

From himself.

From the memories that haunted him.

Four

Avoidance.

It was a method of coping that Alayna had dealt with successfully on both a personal and a professional level. Her familiarity with this particular technique had made it easy for her to recognize Jack's use of it. She'd even hoped to convince him that avoidance resolved nothing, that talking was a much healthier way of dealing with his problems.

And now, here she was, contemplating using the avoidance technique herself…and with Jack, no less.

She sighed and tucked the bedspread neatly beneath her pillow, then straightened, her gaze going unerringly to the bedroom window. She caught her bottom lip between her teeth and worried it as she stared at Jack's cabin nestled beneath the grove of live oaks in the distance. Early-morning sunlight turned the old tin roof to pewter beneath the shade of the old oaks.

But how on earth could she avoid Jack when he worked for her? When his work required him to be in her home, right beneath her very nose, under her feet?

"Alayna!"

She jumped guiltily, then turned. "In here, Billy!" she called and headed for the door. She met both him and Molly in the hall and forced a smile for them. "All ready for school?" she asked as she knelt to adjust the ribbons she'd placed in Molly's hair.

Molly bobbed her head, held out her teddy bear as proof, then quickly tucked it under her arm again. Smiling, Alayna gave her a hug and a kiss, then stood, turning to Billy. He eyed her warily. "Did you remember to pack your math assignment?" she asked him.

He rolled his eyes. "Yeah."

"Yes, ma'am," Alayna corrected as she placed her hands firmly on his shoulders and gave him a turn.

His shoulders rose and fell with a frustrated sigh beneath her hands. "Yes, ma'am," he muttered.

Biting back a smile, Alayna peeked inside his backpack to make sure the assignment was there, then zipped the cover. Before he could move away from her, she spun him around and gave him a quick hug and kiss before he could duck free. "Gotcha," she said, laughing.

Billy dragged the back of his hand across his cheek. "Gross," he complained.

"You love it and you know it," Alayna teased.

Molly giggled when Billy rolled his eyes again and Alayna shot her a conspiratorial wink. A horn sounded out front and Alayna hustled the two down the hall and out the front door. She stood in the doorway and waved to Jaime, Mandy's son, who waited in the truck out front. "Have a good day," she called to them as they climbed into the cab.

"Yeah, right," Billy muttered and slammed the door.

Chuckling softly, Alayna closed the front door, then sagged back against it with a sigh. The peaceful silence in the house slowly settled over her.

But the sense of peace was only temporary. She still had Jack to deal with. The children's departure for school served as a reminder that he would be arriving at any moment.

His attitude toward the children concerned her. Not that he was mean to them, or anything. He just—well, he simply ignored them. Even at the dinner table each night, he erected this invisible wall around himself that prevented Billy or Molly from drawing too close. Not that the wall was necessary, considering the amount of time Jack spent in their presence. He all but choked down his dinner, then would excuse himself and hightail it for the cabin as quick as he could.

He avoided them.

Just as she wanted to avoid him.

She sighed again and headed for the kitchen mentally kicking herself for her cowardice. She knew she couldn't avoid Jack any more than she could avoid acknowledging her own shortcomings. What had happened on the pier the night before was her fault, not his. Jack was a man, after all. A full-blooded, all-American man, and it was only natural that he'd have a man's appetite for sex.

The problem was that she was only half a woman.

No, she argued silently, giving her head a shake. She wasn't half a woman. She had all the necessary parts. Even the emotions and desires to go with them. But there was a short circuit somewhere. Some fluke of nature that resulted in a malfunction. To put it simply, her parts, when put into motion simultaneously, just didn't work.

And it was better to admit the failing, than to pretend otherwise.

She'd arrived at that conclusion months ago when her divorce from Alex had become final. At the same time, she'd decided that she could lead a full and happy life alone, without the companionship or intimacy found with a man.

But what she hadn't realized was that while she might be able to intellectually and physically choose to live her life without a man, she couldn't sever her desire for one.

Jack had certainly proved that.

The night before, on the pier, she'd wanted to make love with him. She'd wanted to feel his hands on her bare skin. To feel the texture of his lips moving on hers. To taste him. Touch him. To have him fill her with...

Groaning, she stumbled to a stop before the kitchen door, and pressed the heel of her hand to her forehead, forcing back the memories, the sensations that had flooded her mind, her body, at his touch. Oh, God, how was she ever going to face him again after what she'd experienced? After she'd made such a fool of herself?

She jerked her hand to her side, curling her fingers into a tight fist, and willed back the unwelcome fears.

Knowing that she had no choice but to face him and to apologize to him, she stepped into the kitchen. She set the skillet on the stove, turned on the burner beneath it, then went to the refrigerator. Eggs. Milk. Butter. She gathered ingredients, refusing to let her thoughts stray from the task at hand. She'd make him a nice breakfast, she told herself. And while they ate, she'd explain why she'd reacted the way she had the night before. She'd tell him why she'd pulled away from him, when what she'd really wanted to do was to make wild, passionate love with him. She'd tell him—

"Alayna?"

The milk carton hit the floor first, followed quickly by the eggs and stick of butter. Alayna stared at the mess spreading at her feet, the cracked eggshells a vivid reminder of her own imperfections. Slowly she lifted her head. Jack stood in the doorway, his cap squeezed between his hands. Without either of them mentioning it, the memory of the night before stretched between them, larger and more humiliating in the light of day. She saw it in his face, in the tightness of his lips, in the regret that shadowed his eyes…in the reluctance that kept him at the door and from drawing any closer to her.

Faced with her inadequacies and the ramifications when she chose to ignore them, she dropped her gaze. "You startled me," she murmured, then sank to her knees, and began to scrape at the milk and eggs with her bare hands. "Sorry about the mess. I'll cook your breakfast as soon as I get it cleaned up."

Tears blinded her and she swiped her wrist beneath her eyes to clear them away, then frantically started scraping again at the spilled milk and broken eggs.

A hand closed around her wrist.

"I'm the one who should be apologizing, Alayna. Not you."

She dipped her chin to her chest and closed her eyes, willing him to disappear, to spare her any more humiliation, any further embarrassment. But when she opened her eyes, his knee was still inches from her own, his fingers still wrapped tightly around her wrist. "It's not your fault," she said and sniffed. "I'm just clumsy, is all."

"Not about the milk," he said, his voice sharp with frustration. "I'm sorry about last night. I—"

Alayna sucked in a breath, knowing if she didn't say

it now and quickly, she never would. She eased free of his grasp, drawing away from him, both physically and emotionally. "It's not your fault," she said and had to fight to keep the quiver from her voice. "I shouldn't have let things go so far." She pushed to her feet and crossed to the sink and tore a length of paper towel from the dispenser. Grabbing a bowl, she returned and dropped down beside him again. She blotted up the pools of milk and, at the same time, managed to keep her face hidden from him.

"Why?"

At the one-word question, her fingers stilled, then she started frantically mopping up the milk again, her movements as jerky as the nerves that jumped beneath her skin. "Because I'm not any good at sex. I know that, but—" She fisted the paper into a wad within her hand, then set her jaw and started scrubbing furiously at the floor. "I just got carried away for a minute. That's all. It won't happen again."

Dumbfounded, Jack stared at the back of her head. She'd lost him right after the part where she'd said she wasn't any good at sex. "You're not any good at sex."

He said it as a statement, not a question, but Alayna felt obligated to respond. "No, I'm not."

"And what makes you think that?"

She stopped her mopping and shot him a frown over her shoulder. "Past experience." She snapped her head back around and continued cleaning.

His mind churning with a thousand questions, Jack watched her, but soon found his thoughts drifting to her backside and how with her kneeling and stretched out so far, wiping up the mess she'd made, her bottom stuck way up in the air. Heart-shaped, each cheek about the size of the spread of his hand, her bottom swayed from side to side in rhythm with the movements of her hand.

Jack slowly shook his head, remembering the way she'd responded to him the night before, and wondered where she'd gotten such a crazy notion. Not any good at sex? Somebody had done a number on this woman, he decided. There was no other explanation. He'd be willing to bet his truck that she was not only *good* in bed, but she was *great*. A woman with as much heart and compassion as Alayna would have to be. "Well, you sure as hell had me fooled."

She sniffed indignantly. "I'm not a tease, if that's what you're thinking."

"I wasn't thinking that at all." He shifted his weight from the balls of his feet to plant one foot solidly on the floor. He braced a forearm along his thigh. "In fact, I was thinking just the opposite."

Opposite? Alayna slowly straightened, sinking back on her heels. She turned to look at him, her curiosity getting the better of her. "And what would the opposite be?"

His eyes lit with a devilish grin. "That you are one hot babe."

Alayna's mouth dropped open. "One hot babe," she repeated, her eyes wide with disbelief.

He slapped a palm against his thigh and pushed himself to his feet. "Yep. One hot babe."

Alayna stared up at him for a full three seconds, her heart racing, her hopes soaring. One hot babe? Could it be true? All those years she'd thought— No, she told herself. Jack was wrong. She knew her sexual abilities better than he did. He'd had—what? All of five minutes on which to base his assessment? She'd had years. Frustrating and heartbreaking years to discover her inadequacies, to have them thrown in her face.

She snorted. *One hot babe.* "Yeah, right," she muttered. She slapped the wad of soggy paper towels into the bowl and stood, chuckling at the ridiculousness of his suggestion as she crossed to the sink. "What would you like for breakfast?"

Though Jack was tempted to push the subject of her sexual prowess, he decided it might be best—for both their sakes—to just let it drop. He didn't want to get involved with her, and she certainly didn't need the complication of getting involved with a man like him. "Those scrambled eggs you were whipping up on the floor looked pretty good to me."

Alayna spun. "Oh, but I can't serve you food that's been—" Then she saw the glint in his eyes, and realized he was teasing her. The tension slowly eased from her shoulders, and she laughed, relieved to know there would be no lingering awkwardness from the previous night's fiasco…and equally delighted to discover that he had a sense of humor buried beneath that gruff exterior.

"Scrambled eggs, it is," she agreed with a decisive nod. She shot him a wink, smiling. "Though I think I'll start with fresh ingredients."

Dust motes danced in the shaft of sunlight coming through the attic window, stirred by Alayna's steps. She stopped beside an old harvest table and pulled back a corner of the drop cloth that covered it, smoothing a hand over the stained wood she'd exposed. She smiled wistfully, remembering meals shared with her family gathered around the table. She didn't know the table's age, but suspected it was well over sixty years old. Maybe even older. She vaguely remembered her father mentioning that the table had once belonged to his grandmother. She didn't know when the table had been relegated to the attic, but suspected that her mother had ordered it stored there when she had redecorated the house over twenty years ago. Alayna bit back a smile, thinking of her mother. Ophelia McCloud had hated the Double-Cross Heart Ranch and the family's required summer visits there. The house was old, she'd complained to her husband, with few amenities, and certainly lacking in refinement. And there was nothing to do in the country, she liked to remind him, but watch the grass grow. To appease her, Alayna's father had allowed his wife to completely redecorate the Pond House. The project had kept her busy for two years—and stopped her complaining for almost that long.

Alayna chuckled. In spite of her parents' differences, they loved each other, sharing that love with their children. And Alayna wanted to continue that legacy by sharing her love with children who had never known love as she had.

She stepped back, studying the long table, already imagining her own brood of children gathered around it. There would be laughter and teasing, and plenty of love to pass around.

"Alayna!"

"Up here," she called. She quickly wiped her palm down her thigh, cleaning off the dust she'd gathered, feeling as if she'd been caught skipping school. When she'd slipped off to the attic, she'd left Jack alone to work on a loose spindle on the staircase banister. That he would seek her out was yet another indication that what had transpired between the two of them on the pier the night before had left no adverse effects, and for that she was thankful.

At the sound of his steps on the stairs, she turned, smiling.

He stopped with one foot planted on the top step and braced his hands on either side of the door frame. He leaned forward, peering inside the room. "What are you doing up here?" he asked, frowning.

The bulge of biceps was impossible for Alayna to ignore. That and the way his jeans hugged his thigh. And the endearing manner in which his hair fell across his forehead was, to her, simply irresistible. She told herself it was merely a motherly instinct that made her want to cross to him, comb the dark hair aside and place a kiss on his forehead to erase the frown lines there.

Thankfully she was honest enough to recognize the excuse for what it was—a lie. She may not be able to have sex with a man, she reminded herself, but she certainly still found them attractive. Especially, it seemed, this particular man.

"Looking for treasure," she replied. She laughed at Jack's startled expression. "Furniture," she clarified. "Things I might be able to use downstairs."

"Oh." He pushed from the doorway and stepped inside the low-ceilinged room. He lifted the corner of a dust cloth and raised a brow. "Nice stuff. Old, but nice." He dropped the cloth. "Do you want me to haul anything down for you?"

Alayna turned to the table, studying it closely, while Jack crossed to stand beside her. "I'd like to take this down, if you think we could manage it."

He fitted his hands around the table's edge and lifted, testing its weight. "I don't know," he said doubtfully. "It's pretty heavy. Might need help with this one." He squatted down, peering beneath it. "We might be able to take the legs off. Would make moving it easier." He stood and tossed back the rest of the cover for a better look.

Alayna gasped, covering her mouth with her hands. "Oh, no," she murmured, reaching to press her fingertips against the buckled wood he'd exposed.

Jack glanced up at the rafters overhead. "Roof must've leaked," he said. "I'll give it a look later." He lowered his gaze to the damaged wood again, shaking his head with regret. "A shame, too."

"Do you think it can be repaired?"

Jack heard the hopefulness in Alayna's voice, and suspected she'd had her heart set on using the table. He stepped closer, rubbing a hand along the damaged wood, praying it wasn't as bad as he'd first thought. "I'm no professional regarding furniture," he said hesitantly, "but I'd think it'd be cheaper to replace it, than to try to repair it. But if you want, I can haul it into town and get an expert's opinion."

She sighed heavily. "No. I trust your opinion." She touched his hand by way of thanking him for the offer, then turned away, as if looking at the table pained her somehow.

Though her touch was fleeting, Jack felt the warmth of it seep deep beneath his skin. It came perilously close to touching his heart. He stared after her, fighting the feelings of compassion she stirred within him, and the almost overwhelming desire to pull her into his arms and just hold her.

At the door, she gestured to a small stack of items she'd piled there. "I'll just take these things for now." She lifted a box and started down the stairs, her shoulders drooped despondently.

Jack glanced back at the table, frowning, wondering what it was about the old table that had made her look as if he'd broken her heart when he'd told her it wasn't worth refinishing. He lifted a shoulder and turned away, heading for the stairs. *Don't let it matter,* he told himself. *You've got troubles enough of your own.*

From the pile of things she'd left stacked by the door, he selected a small rocker, then followed her down the narrow stairway.

Jack cocked his head, listening. When he didn't hear the sound again, he went back to his sanding. He wasn't sure if he could save the table Alayna had unearthed in the attic, but he was going to give it his best shot. He'd had the truck driver, who had delivered the tin he'd ordered to repair the roof, help him haul the table to the barn. Alayna, who at the time had been in town buying groceries, was unaware that he'd raided her attic. He planned to keep her in the dark until he determined whether or not he could save the old table.

As he sanded and smoothed the buckled wood, he tried to convince himself that he wasn't doing the work to please Alayna. He was a man who loved wood, no matter what the form, and hated to see it go to waste.

He straightened, flexing his cramped fingers. "Yeah right, Cordell," he muttered. "You're a sucker for a sad face. Especially when it's attached to a pretty woman. You always were."

Frowning, he bent to his task again, putting muscle behind the steady movements of his hand.

And heard the sound again.

Lifting his head, he listened. Sure enough, the sound came again. This time, though, he set aside the round of coarse steel wool and stepped outside and into the darkness.

"Here, kitty-kitty-kitty."

Molly? He squinted against the darkness, trying to make out her small form in the moonless night. He saw a flash of white near the front porch of the Pond House and headed that way. He found the girl kneeling in front of the broken lattice that screened the crawl space beneath the porch, her face pressed again the dark opening.

"Molly?"

She jumped at the sound of his voice and rolled to her back, bracing herself with hands planted on the soft grass behind her.

Jack frowned at the fear he saw in her eyes. The kid hadn't said two words to him the entire time he'd been living on the place. She just stared at him, her eyes wide and watchful, her body poised for flight in case he made a wrong move.

And that made Jack mad. He didn't want to scare the kid...but then he didn't want her to like him, either. A hell of a situation, in his estimation.

He glanced toward the house, thinking he'd just get Alayna and let her deal with the kid. Then the cat meowed again, and Molly made a whimpering sound that had Jack whipping his head back around. The look of fear was still in her eyes, but so was her concern for the cat. With a sigh, Jack dropped to a knee in front of the girl, hoping that by putting himself on her level he'd reduce her fear somewhat.

But she remained frozen, her eyes wide and full of fear.

"What are you doing out here in the dark?" he asked. "Shouldn't you be in bed?"

She didn't say a word. Didn't even blink. She just stared at him as if he was some kind of monster who was going to gobble her up for his supper.

He bit back a sigh of frustration. "Does Alayna know you're out here?"

She wagged her head and dug her heels in the ground, inching away from him.

Meow-w-w.

Molly flopped to her stomach at the pitiful sound and pressed her face against the dark opening in the lattice.

Jack lowered himself to the ground and eased up beside her. He squinted against the darkness. "Is that Captain Jinx?" he asked, turning to look at Molly.

She bobbed her head in assent. "He hurts," she said, pointing a stubby finger at the hole in the lattice.

Shocked that the child had actually spoken to him, Jack peered at her more intently. "How do you know?"

"Heard him cryin'."

Jack turned his face back to the hole. He stared into the darkness, but couldn't see a thing. He rolled to his side, and worked a penlight from the pocket of his jeans. Molly jerked away from him at the unexpected movement.

"It's a light," he explained, and flicked it on and off, demonstrating. "See?"

She watched him warily. With a frown he rolled back to his stomach. He inched his way to the hole and shined the light into the crawl space. The light glanced off a matched pair of eyes, glinting like green marbles in the darkness. Cat eyes. He adjusted the beam, aiming it along the animal's length. Ugly and scraggly before, the critter looked a whole lot worse now. It's fur was matted with blood and one ear hung by threads of skin. Probably found another stray tom and got himself into a fight, Jack reasoned.

He felt a movement beside him and turned quickly, blocking Molly's view of the injured cat. "Molly," he said, firmly taking her by the shoulders. She stiffened and tried to pull away from him, but he tightened his grip, hating the fear he saw in her eyes. "Captain Jinx is hurt," he explained gruffly. Her gaze shot to the darkened hole, her lips trembling. He squeezed her shoulders and she slowly turned back to him. Tears glistened in her brown eyes. Jack had to swallow back the emotion that rose at the sight. "I want you to go and get Alayna. Tell her to bring me a towel. Can you do that?"

She bobbed her head and ducked from his grasp, scrambling to her feet and running for the house. Her white nightgown flapped around her short legs.

Jack quickly ripped off his shirt, knowing he had to get the cat out before Molly saw it. Wedging his fingers between the lattice and the wooden steps it was attached to, he pulled, gritting his teeth and straining until the weathered panel of lattice snapped free with a splintering of wood.

Breathing heavily, he tossed the panel aside and crawled inside the darkened hole, flattening his stomach against the dank-smelling earth in order to fit into the narrow space. "Okay, cat," he muttered, belly-crawling toward it, "try to remember that I'm here to help you, okay?"

In answer, Captain Jinx bared his teeth and hissed, swiping at Jack with his sharp claws.

"Yeah, well, I'm not too crazy about you, either," he muttered darkly, then tossed his shirt over the cat. He scooped the netted cat under his arm, trying his best to be gentle and not injure the cat any more than it already was, then slowly started backing his way from the hole. The cat scratched and clawed, trying to get free.

Jack felt a hand on his foot and froze.

"Jack?"

"Yeah," he said on a sigh of relief, recognizing the

sound of Alayna's voice. "I've got the cat. Where's Molly?"

"In the house. I made her stay with Billy."

"Good idea." His shoulders cleared the opening, then his head, and he rolled to his back, holding the squirming cat against his chest, as he gulped in a breath of fresh air. Someone turned on the porch light, probably Billy he reasoned, and he squinted against the sudden glare.

Alayna bent over him, her blond hair falling to curtain her face, her blue eyes filled with concern. Her eyes suddenly widened and she dropped to her knees beside him.

"Oh, Jack," she cried, laying a sympathetic hand against his abdomen. "You're bleeding."

He shifted the now calm cat to one arm and craned his neck to see, then dropped his head back to the ground. "It's just a scratch."

He thought she'd remove her hand once he'd assured her he wasn't hurt, but she kept it there. Her palm smoothed across his bare flesh, brushing away the dirt and awakening nerves beneath the skin. Though her touch was light, tender, filled with compassion, for some crazy reason Jack found its movements highly erotic.

She hadn't touched him since that night on the pier—other than that brief contact in the attic—and Jack hadn't made a move to touch her, either. Didn't dare. They just danced around each other like boxers avoiding the next punch.

But she was touching him now.

He lay still as death, cussing himself for a fool in one breath for not brushing her hand away, and praying with the next that she'd never stop her hand's seductive play. She continued to stroke him, her palm shaping the hardened lines of muscle, smoothing across the taut, flat plane of his stomach, slipping over his side, then starting the journey all over again.

When her fingertips dipped into the shallow well of his navel, Jack couldn't stop the groan of pleasure that swelled from deep inside him, any more than he could prevent his abdominal muscles from tightening in response to her finger's erotic play.

Her gaze snapped to his at the movement. Jack felt the heat that burned between them, saw the need that turned her blue eyes to smoke.

Though he knew it was a mistake, he reached and covered her hand with his free one. "Alayna."

I'm not any good at sex. He could see the words in her eyes as clearly as if they were written there. He remembered the morning she'd told him that. Obviously she remembered that morning, too, because she dropped her gaze from his, her cheeks flushed in embarrassment.

"I'm sorry," she whispered and withdrew her hand from beneath his to curl it into a fist on her thigh.

She drew in a ragged breath. "How bad is Captain Jinx?"

Jack wanted to tell her that it was okay to touch him, to beg her to touch him again. But refrained. Neither of them needed the complication. Instead he took the distraction she offered. If it was the coward's way out, so be it. Jack wasn't there to win any medals. "I'm no vet, but I'd say he's pretty bad off. Not unfixable. Just bad."

She pushed herself to her feet, still avoiding his gaze. "I'll call Sam. My cousin. She's a vet."

Jack winced and turned his back to the makeshift table where the vet worked a suture through the cat's tattered flesh, reattaching its ear. The cat was anesthetized. Probably didn't feel a thing. But Jack felt every prick of the needle as if it was piercing his own skin.

"You're Mandy's sister, right?" he asked, needing to take his mind off of what was going on behind his back.

"Yep. And Merideth's. I don't think you've met her yet."

Jack stole a glance over his shoulder, winced again as the needle pierced the cat's flesh, and turned his face away.

"You gonna faint on me?"

Jack chuckled at the question and wagged his head. "No. Just don't ask me to help."

"I'm used to working alone."

Jack nodded, but didn't dare turn back around. "The cat's going to be okay, isn't it? I mean, it would break Alayna's heart if he didn't make it. The kid's, too."

"He'll make it. Not without a few new scars, but he'll make it."

Jack felt as if a hundred pound weight had been lifted from his shoulders. He may not care for cats, but that didn't mean he wanted the animal to suffer…or the humans who cared for it, for that matter. He frowned as his thoughts shifted to Alayna.

He remembered the hand on his abdomen, the needs it had drawn, the look of embarrassment on her face when she realized that she had kept her hand on his flesh a moment too long. He remembered, too, the yearning he'd seen in her eyes before she'd turned her face away. He didn't want her to suffer, but something told him that she already had. Probably at the hand of her ex-husband.

He glanced over his shoulder again at Sam's bent head and decided she might just be the one to answer a few of the questions he had about Alayna's past.

"Alayna told me that she's divorced."

"Yep."

"Did you know her husband?"

"Yep."

Jack rolled his eyes. Getting information out of the woman was like pulling teeth.

He tried again. "She seems to have a few hang-ups about—well, what I mean to say is that her self-confidence seems to be lacking in certain areas."

"If you're asking me if her husband was an asshole, yeah, he was."

Jack turned, then grimaced when he saw that Sam had opened up the wound on the cat's side and was cleaning it. The woman must have a stomach of iron. He swallowed back the bile that rose to his throat and shifted his gaze to a spot on the barn wall above her head. "What'd he do to her?"

Sam's head snapped up, her gaze slamming into his. To Jack, it was like running headfirst into a steel wall.

"Why do you ask?" she asked suspiciously.

Jack shrugged. "Just curious."

Frowning, she turned her attention back to the cat. "Why don't you ask Alayna?"

He shrugged again, though she didn't see the uneasy gesture. "Didn't want to embarrass her."

Sam tossed the clamp aside with its square of soiled gauze and picked up her sutures. "Neither do I," she replied tersely, and bent back over her work.

Jack was sure that was all she was going to offer on the subject, but then she glanced up at him, her eyes narrowed, her mouth set in a grim line. "You ever see a woman who's been physically abused?"

Jack slowly nodded. "Yeah. Pictures."

"Well, that's how Alayna looked after her divorce. And he did it without ever laying a hand on her." She tapped a finger to her head. "Did it here," she said. "Played with her mind. Made her think she wasn't much of a woman." She wagged her head, scowling. "She's one of the smartest, warmest, most compassionate women I've ever known, and pretty to boot. He had her convinced she was none of those things."

Jack worked alone the next day. Although Alayna had left him a note, telling him that she had business to attend to in town, he suspected that she was avoiding him.

He couldn't say that he blamed her. She was probably embarrassed by her actions the night before. He was still having a hard time believing what Sam had told him about Alayna's past. Not that he doubted the truth in what she had shared. It was just difficult for him to believe that a woman like Alayna would fall prey to emotional abuse—but then he figured it was probably all those wonderful traits of hers that had made her a prime target. Warm, loving, compassionate. The whole time her ex was dishing out the abuse, Alayna had probably been dancing a jig, trying her damnedest to please him.

He sighed and tossed his hammer aside. It clattered musically against the tin roof he was mending. Don't let her get to you, Jack, he warned himself. Do your job and hit the road. Chase that white line.

Pressing his hands to the small of his back, he straightened his spine, easing out the kinks. Sweat dampened his shirt beneath his hands, making it stick to his back as he looked out at the road that led to the Pond House.

In the distance, he saw a cloud of dust appear, chasing a fast-moving vehicle. Not a minivan, though, he noted, and tried to ignore the stab of disappointment that came. It was a truck. School was out. The kids were coming home.

And Alayna was nowhere in sight.

Which left Jack in charge. And he didn't want to be in charge, he thought as panic set in. He didn't want the responsibility, the closeness that required.

He quickly started gathering his tools, hoping to make it to his cabin before they arrived, but the truck braked to a dust-churning stop just as he stepped down from the ladder he'd propped against the roof's edge. The truck's passenger door swung open, the kids piled out, the door slammed again and the truck made a wide U-turn, its driver honking as he accelerated in the opposite direction.

Jack felt the trapdoor slam shut in his face. Like it or not, he was caught.

Molly raced across the lawn, her cheeks flushed, her pigtails bobbing, that damn bear of hers tucked tightly under her arm. She skidded to a stop in front of Jack and peered up at him, her eyes wide and questioning. "Kitty?" she asked breathlessly.

That she would approach him, speak directly to him, caught Jack off guard. He nodded toward a box tucked up by a support post on the front porch, in the shade. She clambered up the steps, dropped to her knees beside the box, peered inside, then looked back at Jack over her shoulder. A smile stretched from ear to ear. "Kitty," she repeated, her voice heavy with relief. She hopped up and skipped down the steps headed straight for Jack. He stiffened as wafer-thin arms clamped around his knees. His heart knotted in his chest, his breath burned in his lungs.

And Molly clung.

Slowly he dipped his chin and stared at the halo of blond hair pressed against his thigh. Slower still, he lifted a hand to cover it. He smoothed his palm across the top of the child's head, the calluses on his fingers snagging on the fine, blond strands. "He's going to be fine," he assured her, his voice husky. "Sam took good care of him."

"Where's Alayna?" Billy stood about six feet away, scowling.

Jack carefully unwound Molly's arms from around his legs and set her aside. She immediately ran back to the box and knelt beside it. "In town," he replied, picking up his toolbox again.

"She comin' back?"

Jack heard the uncertainty in the boy's voice, though his face revealed nothing but his dislike for Jack. "Yeah. She'll be back."

"When?"

"Don't know."

Billy tossed his backpack to the ground and Jack could almost hear the wheels turning in the kid's head. Freedom. Nobody in charge. He wondered how much trouble the kid could get himself into before Alayna returned. Plenty, Jack suspected.

Knowing he was the only adult around to stand between Billy and a full-scale rebellion, Jack tried to think of what Alayna would do if she were home. "Take your school things to your room," he said, improvising, "and start on your homework."

"I don't have to do what you say."

"Yeah, you do," Jack returned.

"Why?"

"'Cause I'm bigger than you."

Billy eyed Jack a moment as if weighing his options, then shrugged. "Okay." He stooped and hooked a finger in the loop of his backpack, dragging it from the ground and to his shoulder. "Come on, Molly."

Jack watched the two disappear inside the house, and narrowed his eyes in suspicion. The kid was up to something. What, he wasn't sure. But something. If he wasn't, Jack figured that the boy would still be standing in the yard debating Jack's right to give him orders. The kid was that stubborn.

Jack headed for the ladder again, cussing Alayna for leaving him in the lurch with one breath and, with the next, praying she'd come home before the kid tried a fast one on him.

Five

Jack heard the back door open and scooted up to the roof's ridge and looked over in time to see Billy tiptoeing across the flagstone patio below. From his vantage point on the Pond House's roof, Jack had a bird's-eye view of the grounds and the kid's every move. He muttered a curse as he watched the boy dart a quick look behind him before he hightailed it for the barn, then disappeared behind it.

The kid was up to something. And probably no good, Jack concluded with a frown. He turned away and picked up a piece of tin, angling it into place on the roof. It wasn't his problem, he told himself as he worked his hammer free from the loop on his tool belt. He was a carpenter, hired to do a remodeling job, not a damn baby-sitter. He upended a nail over the tin and quickly hammered it into place.

And glanced in the direction of the barn again.

What was the kid doing sneaking around, anyway? he wondered irritably. He ought to be in the house doing his homework, as Jack had instructed.

After more than a week living a little less than a hundred yards away, Jack knew Alayna's and the kids' routine by heart. He'd made it his business to know their schedule so that he could avoid the kids as much as possible. The only time he saw them was at dinner, and then just long enough for Jack to choke down enough food to appease Alayna and then split.

According to the schedule he'd witnessed, the kids should be in their rooms doing their homework, and Alayna should be in the kitchen preparing their dinner.

But Alayna wasn't home.

"Damn!" he muttered under his breath.

He eased to the ridge of the roof for another look at the barn. His eyebrows shot up. Was that smoke? He squinted against the sunlight to see better. Damn him for a blind man, if it wasn't, he cursed silently, recognizing the thin threads of smoke as they curled around the side of the barn.

Setting his jaw, he headed for the ladder and quickly climbed down from the roof, then stalked angrily for the barn. Just before he reached the rear of the building, he lightened his steps, wanting to take the kid by surprise. He hoped to scared the hell out of the little brat. Pleased with the image that thought drew, he eased to the side of the barn and peeked around the corner.

Billy sat with his back against the weathered wood, a cigarette clamped between his fingers, blowing smoke through puckered lips. A pack of cigarettes lay on the ground beside him and a box of kitchen matches lay just beyond.

Jack stepped around the corner. "Didn't know you smoked."

Billy was on his feet and had his hand behind his back before Jack took the next step.

He lifted his chin and eyed Jack defiantly. "Who said I did?"

Jack had to choke back a laugh. The kid had balls, that was for sure. With smoke curling up from behind him, the evidence on the ground at his feet, he *still* wanted to deny his guilt.

Jack dropped to his haunches, turned his back to the barn wall and sat down, stretching his legs out in front of him. "Nobody." He picked up the pack of cigarettes and tossed them in his hand. "Just saw these cigarettes and figured they were yours."

"I didn't steal 'em, if that's what you're thinkin'."

Jack lifted a shoulder. "Didn't say you did."

Billy eased closer, prepared to run if the situation called for it. "I bought 'em from a kid at school. Used my lunch money."

Jack looked up at him. "How much did you pay?"

"Three bucks."

Jack whistled through his teeth at the hefty price, then lifted the lid on the box and looked inside. Less than half a pack remained. "You smoked half a pack, already?"

When it appeared that Jack wasn't going to whip him or knock him around like the other men in his life probably had done, Billy sank down onto the ground beside him, but still kept an arm's length between them. Just in case.

"Nah. The kid only had half a pack." He held out the half-smoked cigarette for Jack's inspection and grinned sheepishly. "This is my first one."

Jack nodded toward the cigarette. "You know those things'll stunt your growth, don't you?"

Billy snorted. "Yeah, yeah. That's what you grown-ups say about everything that's cool."

Jack shook out a cigarette from the pack. "Mind if I have one?"

Sensing a comrade in crime, Billy relaxed a little more. He gave his shoulder a lift, much like he'd seen Jack do earlier. "Sure, dude. Why not?"

Jack clamped the cigarette between his teeth, then let it dangle there while he reached for the matches. He flicked his fingernail across the head of one and a flame flared to life.

Billy's eyes widened in awe. "Cool, dude. How'd you do that?"

Cupping his hands around the flame, Jack touched it to the end of the cigarette, then stuck the match into the dirt, snuffing it out. "I don't know," he said with a shrug. "Just a trick I picked up." He took a drag on the cigarette, but was careful not to inhale. He didn't want to choke in front of the kid. He had a lesson to teach, one his own father had taught him years ago.

He shook out another cigarette and offered it to Billy. "Want another one?"

Billy eased closer. "Sure, why not?" He poked the cigarette between his lips and held it steady with fingers no longer than the length of the cigarette while Jack struck another match and held it to the cigarette's end. Billy inhaled deeply, then bent double, coughing and choking.

Jack pounded him on the back. "That one have a bone in it?" he teased.

Billy sat up, his eyes watering, then grinned. "Yeah. Guess it did."

They sat for a while, saying nothing, just smoking. Or at least Billy was smoking. Jack wasn't a smoker. He'd learned his lesson the hard way years ago from his old man. The same lesson he was about to give Billy. He just let his cigarette burn, taking a puff now and again just to make himself look as if he was an active participant.

When Billy snubbed his cigarette out in the dirt, Jack handed him another one. Billy's grin was a little weaker this time, and his coloring wasn't quite the same, but he took the offered cigarette with a "Thanks, dude" and puffed away.

Jack watched an army of ants march by, swatted lazily at a fly, then stubbed his burned-out cigarette in the dirt.

"Alayna'd have a wall-eyed fit if she knew we was out here smokin'," Billy said after a bit.

Jack just nodded his head. "Yep. Probably would."

"Kids aren't supposed to smoke, you know," he added as if Jack might not be aware of that fact.

Jack had to turn his head to hide his grin. "I see kids smoking all the time. Some of 'em not any bigger than you." He cocked his head to look at Billy. "How old are you, anyway?"

Billy straightened to make himself look taller. "Seven," he said proudly. "I'll be eight 'fore long."

Jack shook out another cigarette, lit it, then passed it to the kid. Billy accepted it, but a little slower this time. The kid didn't even seem to notice that Jack wasn't smoking. Jack stole a glance at the boy and saw that he was looking a little green behind the gills. "You feeling all right?"

Billy slid a little lower down the wall. "Yeah. I'm okay." He rolled his head to the side and looked up at

Jack. "You aren't gonna tell Alayna that we've been smokin', are you?"

Jack lifted a shoulder. "Don't see why I should."

His reply seemed to relieve Billy somewhat because he rolled his head back around and stared off into the distance. His eyes had a glassy look, and his face was as white as his T-shirt. Maybe whiter, Jack decided, noting the dirt stains.

It won't be long now, Jack thought as he turned his gaze to the distant hills. He felt sorry for the kid, knowing what was coming, but figured it was the best way for the boy to learn that cigarettes weren't good for him. Kids rarely listened to the advice of adults, thinking that their elders were just stupid and old-fashioned. Jack knew, because he'd thought the same thing of his own old man.

Things didn't change much over time, he reflected philosophically. Just your perspective as you grew older.

"Jack?"

"Hmm?"

"I don't feel so good."

Jack turned his head to look at the boy. Tousled brown hair in need of a cut. Faded, baggy jeans with a grass stain on one knee. High-top tennis shoes with their tongues hanging out and their laces untied. An oversize T-shirt with a Chicago Bulls emblem emblazoned on its front. Billy looked like a hundred other kids Jack had seen on the streets, all of them searching for an identity, a place to belong.

His own son would never experience any of those things.

Jack swallowed hard, forcing back the memory, the pain. "What hurts?" he asked, trying to keep an emotional distance from the kid.

Billy let his head slide along the wall until it rested

against Jack's arm. "My stomach," he said miserably. He dropped the half-smoked cigarette to the ground and clutched his stomach. "It feels like the inside of a washing machine. You know, all churnin' and foamy inside."

"Are you going to be sick?"

"I—" Billy lunged forward, falling to his hands and knees and gagging.

Jack scrambled to his feet and grabbed the boy, pulling him to his feet, as well. With one arm looped around the boy's waist, holding him upright, and the other holding the kid's hair from his face, Jack held Billy while he emptied his stomach.

"I'm dyin'," Billy wailed, his fingers digging into the arm Jack had wrapped around his waist to support him. "I—I'm dy-y-ing."

"No, son," Jack soothed. "You aren't going to die. But I bet you won't ever smoke a cigarette again, will you?"

Billy retched again at the mention of cigarettes. "No, oh, jeez, no, I promise. I'll never smoke again."

Jack squatted down beside the boy and lifted a wide hand to smooth the limp hair from the boy's pale, sweat-dampened face. In doing so, he exposed a band of freckles sprinkled across his nose, and a scar on his forehead. Without wanting to, or even knowing why he did it, he pressed his other hand against the boy's chest, feeling the frantic beat of his heart, the warmth of his body. He was alive.

And Jack's son wasn't.

Jack dropped his hand to his knee and curled the ends of his fingers into the taut denim. "You gonna be okay?" he asked, his voice husky.

Billy straightened, drawing in a slow, deep breath, and

tested his lungs, his ability to breathe without puking up his guts again. "Yeah. I think so. I—"

"Billy!"

At the shocked sound of Alayna's voice, both Billy and Jack spun and found her standing by the side of the barn, her eyes wide in alarm.

Her gaze moved from them to the almost empty packet of cigarettes and the stubbed-out butts on the ground. Slowly she lifted her gaze to Jack, her blue eyes dark with accusation. "How could you?" she whispered. "How *could* you!" she repeated in a near scream. She rushed across the distance that separated them and pulled Billy into her arms, and away from Jack, crushing the boy against her.

"But, Alayna," Billy began, his voice muffled by her breasts.

"It's okay, Billy," she soothed, shifting him to her side, but keeping her arm locked protectively around him. "We'll get you to the house and get you cleaned up." With a last scathing look at Jack, she turned, and marched for the Pond House.

Slowly Jack pushed to his feet, watching Alayna all but drag Billy along with her, still feeling the sting of her accusation.

It's better this way, he told himself. Better for her to be angry with him, rather than with the boy. The kid deserved her love and attention, and needed it.

Jack didn't.

But he'd taught the boy a valuable lesson, one his own father had taught him. One he'd never get the chance to teach his own son. One Billy's father should have been around to teach Billy.

But Jack had been there. And he'd delivered the lesson

with the same degree of thoughtfulness and care his own father had expressed when he delivered the lesson to him.

And for that Jack felt a small measure of pride.

"Where's Jack?" Molly asked sullenly.

Alayna had to struggle to keep her gaze from straying to the empty chair at the dinner table. "I guess he isn't hungry tonight."

"Probably hidin' out," Billy grumbled, "after the way you yelled at him. And he didn't even do nothin' wrong."

"Bil-l-ly."

There was just enough I-refuse-to-listen-to-another-word-about-this in the warning to have Billy swelling up like a toad.

"Well, it's the truth," he argued. "He *didn't* do nothin' wrong. I tried to tell you he didn't, but you wouldn't listen, and now he's probably out in that cabin of his starvin' to death 'cause he's afraid to come up here for supper."

Alayna inhaled deeply, then slowly released the breath, fighting for patience...and relief from the guilt.

Billy had told her what had happened. That Jack hadn't supplied the cigarettes, that Billy had bought them from another child at school. How Jack had held him while he'd been sick.

She tried to justify her reaction by telling herself that anyone happening upon the scene would have made the same assumption that she had.

Squaring her shoulders defensively, she picked up a bowl and held it close to Molly's plate, lifting a laden spoon. "Would you care for some more mashed potatoes, sweetie?"

Molly shook her head, her pigtails slapping against her

cheeks. "If Jack's not eatin', I'm not, neither. And neither is Teddy," she added, stubbornly hugging the bear that was perched on her lap to her stomach.

Alayna dropped the bowl to the table, then her elbow beside it and pressed her hand against her aching forehead. Silently she counted to ten.

It's easier to spit out an apology than it is to try to swallow it and choke on the hoarded words.

Alayna groaned as one of her father's favorite country wisdoms came to mind. He had a saying for everything, and no matter how angry or upset she was when he offered them, she eventually had to face their truths.

She lifted her head, pressing her fingers against her lips as she looked from one accusing face to the other. "Okay, okay," she said, dropping her hand and sagging back in her chair in defeat. "I'll go and talk to him."

"You'll tell him you're sorry?" Billy asked pointedly.

Alayna leaned across the table to ruffle his hair. Oddly he didn't dodge the affectionate display. "Yes, I'll tell him I'm sorry."

Molly hopped down from her chair and pressed herself against Alayna's legs, her eyes as wide as saucers. "And you'll take him his supper?"

"Yes," Alayna said, laughing at the child's serious tone. "I'll take him his supper."

With a nod of approval, Molly held out her bear. "Take Teddy, too. Jack might be scared staying all by hisself."

Knowing that the bear was what Molly had clung to on those nights when her mother had left her alone, Alayna had to bite back tears. She took the bear and set him on her lap, then pulled Molly into her arms. "I'm sure Jack will appreciate the company." She drew back and swiped a hand beneath her eye to catch a stray tear.

"Now you two scoot up to your rooms," she ordered sternly, shooing them away with her hand, "and do your homework while I'm gone."

"Yes, ma'am," they replied in unison.

Without a whine or a single complaint, the two headed for the stairs. Alayna watched as Billy slipped a brotherly arm along Molly's shoulder, and heard him whisper, "If you get scared without your teddy, you can come in my room with me."

Alayna dreaded having to face Jack again. Almost as much as she dreaded offering the apology she'd promised the children she'd give him. It seemed as if she was always having to apologize to him for one thing or another. Usually the other, she thought, feeling the familiar heat on her cheeks.

With a groan, she quickened her step. She didn't understand why she was so physically attracted to him. And she certainly didn't understand why she'd touched him so impulsively, so intimately, the night before, especially after she'd made such a fool of herself that night on the pier.

But she had, and then she'd done what she'd sworn she'd never do again. She'd avoided facing him—as well as her inadequacies—by leaving him a note and escaping to town.

But not anymore. No more avoidance.

Firming her lips, she shifted the teddy bear under her arm to free a hand and rapped her knuckles sharply against the cabin's thick oak door. After a moment, the door opened and a shirtless, wet-headed Jack stood in the opening, a damp towel draped around his neck.

The sight of his bare chest and the beads of moisture that clung to the dark hair that covered it were a vivid reminder to Alayna as to why she found Jack so physically attractive. As Maudie would say, he was one good-looking hunk of man.

"What can I do for you?"

Alayna snapped her gaze to his and found the familiar frown on his lips. Her hands trembling a bit, she lifted the covered plate. "A peace offering." When his frown deepened, she held out the teddy bear as added incentive. "Molly sent this. She thought you might be scared to be by yourself." Tears pushed at her throat as she repeated Molly's words, knowing what a sacrifice it was for Molly to offer Jack the bear.

Jack looked at the stuffed animal, then slowly took it, holding it between his hands as if it were a priceless treasure that he might break. "She sent me her bear?"

Unable to trust her voice, Alayna nodded.

Jack shifted his gaze from the bear to Alayna. "But she never turns loose of this thing."

Alayna gave up trying to hold back the tears. "I know," she said, blotting the tears from her cheeks with the heel of her free hand. "That's what makes the gift so precious."

Only then aware of the waterworks that were going on in front of him, Jack stripped the towel from around his neck and traded it for the plate Alayna held. He opened the door wider.

Alayna dabbed at her eyes and her cheeks with the towel, trying to get a grip on her emotions as she passed by him. "Thank you," she murmured gratefully.

Once inside, she took a deep breath, determined to offer the apology that she owed Jack. "I came to apologize for yelling at you today and accusing you wrongly. When I saw you there with Billy and saw those cigarettes on the ground—"

"He has a scar on his forehead."

Startled by the interruption, Alayna turned and saw that Jack had closed the door but was still standing by it, his gaze fixed on the bear. For a moment, she thought he was talking about a flaw on the face of Molly's Teddy...then she realized he was talking about Billy. Wearily she combed her hair back from her face and held it there. "Yes, I know. I've seen it."

"How he'd get it?"

Alayna dropped her hand, letting her hair fall, and sank down onto the sofa, feeling every one of her thirty years. "His father. I didn't know he was the one who put it there until today, though. When I was in town I went by the social worker's office and asked to see Billy's file."

"Why?"

"Because I need to know his history, in order to know how to better help him."

"No, no," Jack said in frustration, turning to look at her, his knuckles white as he tightened his grip on the bear. "Why did his father hurt him?"

Before, she'd thought his eyes empty, lifeless, but at the moment they were full of emotion. Rage, fury, indignation for a boy he claimed to dislike. "I don't know why," she said carefully. "I just know that he did. Several times. Billy was taken away from his parents when he was four. He's spent the last three years in a succession of foster homes."

Still frowning, Jack crossed the room, dropped the plate onto the old trunk that served as a coffee table, then sank down on the sofa beside Alayna. He propped his elbows on his knees, and held the bear out in front of him. "And Molly?" he asked after a moment.

"Her father is listed as 'Unknown' on her birth certificate."

"Her mother?"

Alayna looked from Jack to the bear that seemed to hold him in some kind of trance. She lifted a shoulder. "They don't know. She had a history of disappearing. She would leave Molly alone for days at a time. That's why the authorities were finally called in. This time, though, she didn't return. She's just...gone. No one knows where."

"What will happen to Molly?"

"She'll stay in the system until her mother gets her act together and comes back to claim her."

"If she doesn't?"

Alayna shrugged again. "The courts will rule her an unfit mother, strip her of her paternal rights and Molly will be put up for adoption."

"Will you adopt her?"

Alayna shifted her gaze to the bear and tried to swallow the wad of emotion that rose. "I—I don't know if I'd be offered the opportunity. Rarely are foster parents allowed to adopt the children who have been placed in their care. The social worker made that very clear upfront." She drew in a shuddery breath. "Plus, I'm single. They prefer to place adoptable children in homes with married couples."

Jack sat for a long time staring, then he turned his head to look at Alayna. "How do you do it? How do you let them go?"

The question was a difficult one, one that Alayna tried very hard not to think about. She turned her gaze to her hands and slowly threaded the towel through her fingers. "I don't know, yet. Molly and Billy are the first foster children I've taken in." She drew in a deep breath and forced a smile to her lips before looking at Jack again. "But I'll manage. The children's happiness is what is most important. Until the time arrives when they leave me, I'll fulfill their needs as best I can.''

Jack propped the bear on the coffee table, then turned, angling a leg onto the sofa between them. He stretched an arm behind Alayna on the sofa's back, his brown eyes fixed on her. ''And what about *your* happiness? *Your* needs?''

Alayna kept the smile in place, though it was difficult. ''I'm a big girl. I don't need anyone to look out for me.''

''You'll miss them.''

The tears were close, but she stubbornly kept them at bay. ''Yes, but there will be other children who'll need my care.''

''But you'll still miss them.''

A tear leaked out and ran down her cheek. She swiped at it with the towel, hoping Jack hadn't seen it, then knotted the towel in her hands. ''Yes, I'll miss them.''

''You've got a big heart, Alayna. The kids are lucky to have you.''

His kindness brought the tears closer. They burned her throat and stung her eyes. She opened her mouth to form a glib reply, one that wouldn't reveal the fears and doubts that lurked inside her...then quickly closed it, swallowing the sob that rose instead.

Jack leaned closer, placing a finger beneath her chin and forcing her face to his. ''Alayna?''

She saw something in his eyes that she had never seen before, something she'd never expected to see. Compassion. She crumpled in the face of it.

''Oh, Jack,'' she cried, giving in to the tears, her fears. ''I want so badly to help them, to provide a good home for them.''

''You're doing fine,'' he assured her.

''Am I?'' She didn't wait for an answer, didn't seem

to want one. "You handled the problem with Billy today so much better than I ever could. I'm not even sure how I *would* have handled it if I'd been the one who had caught him smoking."

Jack already had one arm open, resting on the sofa behind her. It seemed only natural to open the other one, too, and offer her a shoulder, the one solid thing he had to give her. When he did, she melted against him on a sob. He stiffened immediately as her body met his, realizing too late that in opening his arms, he'd exposed his chest...his heart.

Slowly he gathered her into his arms, tucking her face into the curve of his neck, and let her cry. Her tears were hot and wet against his bare skin, slowly melting his resistance. He gathered her closer, holding her, murmuring senseless words to soothe her. He understood her tears as few other men could. He'd experienced the grief firsthand. He'd already faced the day where he'd had to say goodbye.

He felt a shudder move through her and dipped his head to look down at her. Her hair formed a golden halo against his bare chest. An angel, he remembered thinking that afternoon when he'd first seen her. Her actions since had only confirmed that first impression. Her care for the children. The kindnesses she'd shown him. The sunny smile with which she greeted every new day. Unable to resist, he pressed his lips against her hair. She forged closer and he felt her breast flatten against his ribs. Their heartbeats became one, beating a single rhythm of shared pain.

Jack sat as still as a statue, giving Alayna the shoulder she needed, the comfort that she deserved, until the muscles in his arm cramped and started to burn.

But he never once moved.

After what seemed like an eternity, a shudder moved through her and vibrated through him. He glanced down, praying that the well had at last run dry.

But looking at her was a mistake. With her face buried in the curve of his neck, her hand curled against his chest, she looked so fragile, so vulnerable, so needy...and somehow so damn right huddled there against him.

Another shudder vibrated through him...but this time it was his own.

He focused on the hand curled against his chest. It was the hand of a lady—long graceful fingers and manicured nails. Yet he knew the strength in those fingers, their willingness to take on any job, no matter how menial. He knew their ability to heal with a compassionate touch.

Slowly he lifted his own hand and laid it over hers, pressing her palm more firmly against his chest. He closed his eyes, curling his fingers around hers, absorbing her warmth, her softness, and tried his damnedest to will her grief, her doubts, away from her and into his own tortured soul.

He felt a shudder run through her and he opened his eyes, needing to see her. "Alayna," he whispered, brushing back the halo of hair that blocked his view of her face. "You're doing just fine. No kid could ask for a better mother, a better home than the one you provide for these kids."

She lifted her face, and sniffed, meeting his gaze with watery, red-rimmed eyes. Jack couldn't remember ever seeing a woman who looked more beautiful.

"Oh, Jack. I want to provide a good home for them. I really do. And I want to believe that what I'm doing for them is right. But I—" She shook her head, her eyes filling with tears again. "I just don't know."

He gave her a reassuring squeeze. "You're doing fine. I give you my word on it."

Alayna laughed softly, then sniffed again. "And we both know how seriously Jack Cordell takes giving his word." She sat up, drawing away from him, and pressed the heels of her hands beneath her eyes, suddenly embarrassed by her emotional display. "I'm sorry," she said, rising to her feet. "I didn't mean to fall apart on you like that. I swear, I'm not normally such an hysterical female."

Already missing her warmth, the comfort of having her body pressed against his, Jack wished like hell he could pull her down on the sofa with him again. But this time they wouldn't be sitting. They'd be stretched-out, their limbs tangled, their bodies meshed. And it wouldn't be comfort and reassurance he'd be giving her. It would be passion, something he doubted her ex, or any other man in her life had ever offered her. "I never thought you were," he said, his voice husky.

She laughed softly and glanced over her shoulder. "Thanks, Jack. For everything." She started for the door.

"Alayna..."

She stopped, stood there with her back to him for what seemed like forever, then slowly turned around. He wondered if it was something in his voice, or if it was that his thoughts were revealed in his eyes. Whichever it was, he knew that she knew exactly what he was asking of her.

He saw the doubts that shadowed her eyes, the internal war being waged. Then she shook her head and backed up a step, and away from temptation. "You're a good man, Jack Cordell. The best. I wish I could—" She paused as if struggling for the words to explain, then tossed up her hands in frustration. "Well, I wish I *could,* but we both know I can't."

By the inflection she placed on the word "could," Jack knew that she was thinking of her inadequacies in the sex department. He knew differently. And he knew, too, that there was only one way to prove it to her.

He stood, prepared to prove it to her, but she spun quickly and headed for the door, cutting him off. "I better get back to the house," she called over her shoulder. "See you in the morning, Jack."

The door closed behind her.

Jack dropped down onto the sofa, staring at the closed door, then fell back, squeezing his eyes shut and digging his fingers through his hair.

Never in his life had he felt more alone, more abandoned than he did at that moment.

He opened his eyes and saw Molly's bear sitting on the trunk. He reached for it and pulled it to his chest, then sat back and waited for the loneliness to fade.

He fell asleep, still waiting.

Six

Jack awakened in the night in a cold sweat, still sitting on the sofa with Molly's bear clutched tight against his chest. With a groan, he tossed the bear aside and scrubbed his hands over his face, trying to figure out what had awakened him.

The answer came quickly, as did the pain. He'd been dreaming again. About his son.

He rose and stumbled his way to the cabin's tiny kitchen. He splashed cold water over his face, trying his best to wash away the memory of his son's face. Sandy-blond hair with a cowlick in the middle of his forehead. A grin that revealed a missing tooth he'd lost prematurely when he'd fallen out of the fort Jack had built him in their backyard. Hands, tiny and curious, that were always busy, that had the power to melt Jack's heart when they were wrapped around his neck.

He groaned and scrubbed harder at his face, then dug

his fingers through his hair as he straightened, as if in doing so he could rip the memories from his mind. He didn't want to remember. He wanted to forget. It was the only way he knew to survive.

Setting his jaw, he braced his hands against the edge of the sink and peered through the kitchen window at the darkness beyond. The Pond House stood in the distance, its windows dark, its occupants sleeping. It's the kids, he told himself, his gaze going to the second-story windows and to the bedrooms where he knew they slept. They were the ones who were keeping the memories alive by reminding him of all he'd lost. Molly with her sweet, cherubic face, and the unselfish gift of her bear. Billy with his devilish pranks and false bravado, his desperate need for a father's guidance.

In spite of Jack's determination to ignore them, they were getting under his skin and dangerously close to his heart.

He shifted his gaze to the first floor, and to the window of Alayna's bedroom. He curled his fingers against the edge of the chipped porcelain sink. The woman who cared for those kids was doing her own part in threatening his sanity. Warm, compassionate, loving. She was beginning to make him yearn for things that could never be.

He had to get out of here, he told himself, and turned away from the window. And the quicker the better.

But first he had to finish the job he'd started.

He'd given his word.

Jack didn't consider himself a thoughtful man, or a generous one, for that matter. The idea of giving a woman a present rarely passed through his mind. But on this particular morning, as he made the short walk to the

Pond House, a gift was what pressed uppermost on his mind. Though the gift he was considering had no monetary value, to his way of thinking, it was priceless.

Before he left, he was going to give Alayna back her sexuality, her self-confidence.

How he was going to go about giving her this gift, he wasn't exactly sure. But he'd figure out a way. He owed her. Well, maybe not him, exactly. The debt wasn't so much his, as it was life's. And life owed her big time.

Alayna was a kindhearted woman, who, in his estimation, had gotten a raw deal. She had a heart filled with love and kindness, and she seemed hell-bent on offering that kindness to every stray that showed up at her door.

Including him.

But what she really wanted—and needed, in Jack's opinion—was a houseful of kids of her own. He knew that she wanted children. She'd told him so herself. But she'd never have those children if she didn't get over this crazy notion that she was no good at sex.

When he approached the kitchen door, he feared there might be an awkwardness between them, considering how the night before they'd touched on that one subject that seemed to cause her so much embarrassment. But she met him at the door with the same smile she had greeted him with every other day since she'd hired him.

"Good morning, Jack!" She held the door wide and looked up at the sky, her eyes shining with appreciation. "Isn't it a beautiful day?"

It could have been storming for all the notice Jack had given the weather. He glanced up to find a clear blue sky, its radiant color broken only by wisps of clouds threaded through. But all he noticed was that the sky was almost the same hue as Alayna's eyes. He dropped his gaze to hers, to verify his assumption. "Yeah. It's beautiful all right."

She waved him in. "You're early. The kids haven't even left for school, yet."

Jack shook his head as he caught the door and followed Alayna inside. He hadn't realized until that moment that she'd been aware of his carefully staged arrivals at the house in order to avoid being around the kids.

He held up the bear. "I thought Molly might want to take Teddy to school with her."

Alayna's lips parted in surprise. "Jack. How sweet. Just a minute," she said, and turned. "Molly!" she called. "Someone is here to see you."

"Who?" But before Alayna could answer, Molly was barreling into the kitchen, her cheeks as pink as the new tennis shoes she wore. Billy was fast on her heels.

Molly skidded to a stop when she saw Jack, her eyes going wide. But this time Jack found no fear in them. He sank down to one knee in front of her and held out the bear. "Thanks, Molly, for the loan."

Hesitantly she reached out to stroke the bear's face. "You can keep him, if you want."

His heart in his throat, Jack pressed the bear into her hands, then crooked a finger to smooth a knuckle against her cheek. "Thanks for the offer, but I think Teddy misses you."

A slow smile spread across Molly's face. "Really?" She held Teddy out and looked at him, her eyes filled with a mixture of love and awe. A horn honked and she quickly tucked the bear under arm. "That's Jaime," she said with a sudden rush of breath. "He hates it if we make him wait." She popped a quick kiss on Jack's cheek, then whirled and raced for the front door. "Bye, Alayna. Bye, Jack," she called over her shoulder.

Billy hooked his backpack over his shoulder. He gave Jack a high five, then grinned. "See ya, dude."

Jack slowly rose, watching the two disappear. "Yeah," he murmured, touching a shaky hand to his cheek and the kiss Molly had left there. "See ya."

Jack worked alongside Alayna throughout the morning, painting one of the upstairs bedrooms—and watched her out of the corner of his eye.

He hung a new clothes rod in the closet he'd enlarged—and frowned at her back.

He snatched up his paintbrush again—and all but screamed his frustration.

He couldn't help himself. The only way he could think to prove to Alayna that she wasn't sexually deficient, was to seduce her, and he wasn't willing to go that far. Besides, even if he was willing, Alayna didn't appear to be the type of woman who would tumble into bed with a man just for the sport of it. And he sure as hell didn't want her drawing any false assumptions from his actions. He cared too much for her to want to do anything that might cause her pain when the time came for him to leave.

And Jack *was* leaving. Just as soon as he finished the remodeling job…and as soon as he figured out a way to give Alayna the gift he wanted to give her.

He glanced her way and frowned. She sure as hell wasn't helping matters any. Throughout the morning, she had worked alongside him all innocence and smiles, telling him stories about her childhood, and throwing in funny little things that Billy and Molly had said or done over the weeks. And the more she talked and smiled, the madder Jack became. How was a man supposed to broach a woman about her sexuality when she was acting like Little Miss Mary Sunshine?

Finally, after three hours of silently stewing, waiting for an opportunity that didn't come, Jack slapped his brush across the top of the open can of paint and left it there.

Alayna turned to peer at him curiously. "Problem?"

"No," he snapped irritably. "Paint's getting thick. Needs some thinner."

He stepped behind her, and out of her line of vision, then folded his arms across his chest and glared at her as she gave her shoulder a "whatever" lift then went back to her painting. For the life of him, he couldn't figure out a way to approach her, or why he felt this undeserved anger toward her. It wasn't as if she *knew* what he was wanting to do.

It's the clothes, he finally decided, needing to put the blame for his anger somewhere. She was wearing a man's tailored shirt again, and those same baggy pants she'd worn the first day they'd worked side by side in the breakfast room.

He frowned as he moved his gaze over the baggy shirt, noting the perspiration that dampened the fabric between her shoulder blades and dotted the bumpy line of her spine. With the air-conditioning off and the open windows letting out paint fumes, but letting in heat, she had to be sweltering under all that garb.

Hell, he was, and he'd stripped off his shirt hours ago!

But then Alayna always wore a lot of clothes, no matter what the temperature. Those stupid, shapeless dresses that covered her from neck to calf. The baggy shirts and pants. Nothing he'd ever seen her in offered a hint to the woman beneath. Well, other than that blue robe of hers, but he didn't figure that counted in the scheme of things, since he'd only seen her in it that one time.

But the fact that she was always covered from neck to toe didn't prevent him from remembering what she felt like beneath all those clothes. The feel of her breast in his hand, small, but firm, her nipple, when aroused, as hard as a ripe berry.

And her taste. He ran his tongue over his upper lip at the memory. Sweet. Innocent. Yet, hot and carnal. An unlikely combination, but there, all the same.

And she considered herself lacking in the sex department. Humph!

He narrowed his eyes at her, wondering if her choice of clothing had anything to do with the image of herself that her ex had left her with.

"Why do you wear so damn many clothes?" The question was out before he realized he'd even intended to voice it.

Startled by his question, she twisted her head around to look at him, then lifted a shoulder and went back to her painting. "Why advertise if you have nothing to sell?"

"Who said anything about advertising or selling? I'd think you'd be more comfortable, not to mention cooler, if you dressed in something with a little less—well, with a little less fabric," he said in frustration.

"I'm comfortable."

"Yeah, and you'd be a hell of a lot more comfortable if you weren't so damn stubborn." He caught her by the shoulder and spun her around. Caught unsuspecting, Alayna dropped her brush and braced her hands against his chest, struggling for balance.

When he reached for the hem of her shirt, her mouth and eyes gaped wide. "What are you doing?" she cried.

"What you won't do." He unbuttoned the bottom four buttons, then quickly caught up the shirt's tails and tied them in a knot under her breasts. He stepped back, eyeing the results, then dipped his hand into his pocket and pulled out his knife.

Her eyes widened even more as she watched him snap open the blade with the flick of a nail. "What are you—"

But before she could fully voice the question, he had a hold of her wrist, pulling her arm out to shoulder level. "Giving you some air." Catching the fabric at her shoulder and holding it out away from her skin, he stuck the knife into the seam and ripped upward, making a good-size slit in the cotton. Ignoring her cry of dismay, he kept a grip on the sleeve while he calmly pressed the backside of the blade against his thigh and closed his knife. He slipped it back into his pocket, then, without warning, gave the sleeve a hard jerk, ripping the fabric and severing the sleeve at the seam.

He felt the shiver that shuddered through her and watched gooseflesh pebble the patch of damp skin he'd exposed to the air. He shifted his gaze to hers, then slowly dragged the sleeve down her arm, watching her blue eyes darken and smolder. He dropped the torn fabric to the floor. "Better?"

With her arm free now, Alayna rubbed a hand up and down it, but was unable to move her gaze from Jack's. Never in her life had she endured anything as sensual, as utterly seductive, as what she had just experienced at his hand. Though he'd exposed only one arm, she felt naked, bare, utterly aroused…and as tongue-tied as a schoolgirl. "Y-yes, th-thank you,"

He lifted his hands to cup her shoulders, and squeezed, his fingers digging into the skin he'd bared. "You can't hide your sexuality," he told her, his voice husky, his brown eyes burning into hers, "any more than you can deny it."

Lost in the emotion that turned his brown eyes almost black, she stared unblinking. She wanted to say something, to do something totally insane, like throw her arms around his neck and kiss him senseless.

But then his hands were gone, and he was turning away, and the opportunity was gone. She closed her eyes and pressed a hand to her throat. Her pulse pounded beneath her shaking fingers.

Oh, God, she cried silently. *Did You send Jack to taunt me with my inadequacies? Or to teach me how to overcome them?*

She opened her eyes in time to hear the back door close behind him.

Oh, how she hoped he was there to teach.

Jack stalked his way to the barn, stepped inside, then slammed the door closed behind him. He grabbed a shovel propped against the wall and hurled it across the room. It hit the far wall with a loud *thunk,* then fell to the ground with a clatter.

But the action didn't relieve Jack's frustration.

"Damn!" he swore, digging his fingers through his hair. "Damn, damn, damn!" He sank to the ground, bracing his elbows on his propped knees, his fingers still knotted in his hair. What had he been thinking? What had made him do such an utterly stupid thing? Grabbing Alayna like that. Ripping her shirtsleeve off.

He heaved a frustrated breath and fell back against the barn wall, dropping his arms to hook them over his knees. Another five seconds and he'd have been kissing her. No, hell, he'd have had her on the floor and been making love to her!

And what a mistake that would've been. With all the hang-ups Alayna had about men and sex, in his present state, Jack would have scared the hell out of her.

And he didn't want to scare her. He didn't want to add to her problems. He wanted to help her. But how? he asked himself. How was he going to help her when every time he looked at her, he wanted to grab her and kiss her senseless?

Think, Cordell, think! he ordered himself. There's got to be a way.

"—then Merideth ran to Daddy and tattled on us and we all got in trouble."

"I did not tattle," Merideth cried indignantly, insulted by Mandy's accusation.

Sam merely laughed.

"Yes, you did," Mandy insisted. "You *always* tattled, didn't she, Alayna?" she asked, turning to her cousin for confirmation.

But Alayna didn't hear the question. She was staring out the kitchen window, her thoughts on Jack back at the house, and remembering the angry look on his face when he'd ripped her sleeve from her shirt, the sensations that had flooded her body when he'd pulled the sleeve down her arm, the huskiness in his voice.

Mandy punched her arm. "Alayna?"

Startled, Alayna snapped her head around. "What?"

"Is something bothering you?"

Alayna's eyes widened. "No!" She sat up straighter in her chair. "I was just—" She shifted her gaze from Mandy's to Sam's and finally to Merideth's, and she saw the doubt in their eyes, and knew that she couldn't fool them. Not her McCloud cousins. They knew her as well as she knew herself. Maybe better. And why would she even try to hide her problems from them when she'd driven over for the sole purpose of seeking their advice? "It's Jack," she admitted reluctantly.

All three cousins leaned forward expectantly. "What about him?"

Alayna plucked at the napkin beneath her glass. "Well, I don't know really. You see—" She huffed a breath, frustrated with her inability to verbalize her current dilemma. "I want to have sex with him," she said bluntly.

Merideth hooted at the ceiling. "Maudie was right. You *did* hire him for his body."

"Merideth!" Mandy and Sam cried in unison.

Merideth lifted her chin. "Men pay for sex. Why can't a woman?"

Laughing, Alayna held up a hand, staving off a sibling battle. Her cousins were so predictable...and so dear. "I wish it were as simple as offering Jack cash and the deed being done." She sank back in her chair with a sigh, her smile fading. "Unfortunately it's not."

Mandy peered at her in concern. "Do you have feelings for him?"

Alayna sat a moment, thinking, knowing Mandy's questions deserved an honest answer. "I don't know," she said at last. "I know I care for him, and I know I'm attracted to him, which is ridiculous considering the amount of time I've known him." She rolled her eyes as soon as the words were out of her mouth. "Know him," she said in exasperation. "I don't *know* anything about him. He stubbornly refuses to discuss his past." She heaved a breath. "I just know what I've witnessed over the last few weeks by living and working so closely with him. And that is," she added pointedly, "that Jack Cordell is a kind and sensitive man—though he tries his best to disguise it. He's honest, extremely knowledgeable about a great number of things and he works very hard.'' She shot Merideth a sly smile. "And he looks pretty darn good without a shirt on, too."

Merideth tossed back her head and laughed, but Mandy's face still registered concern. "What happened between the two of you to provoke this sudden desire to have sex with a man you hardly know?"

Alayna frowned. "Well, this morning," she began, then stopped, shaking her head. "No, actually it began several weeks ago when he kissed me."

"He kissed you?" Mandy repeated, unable to disguise her surprise.

"Yes. It was the night you invited us all for dinner. I was determined to find out why Jack had refused to join us, so after I put the children to bed, I went in search of him. I found him on the pond's pier. We were sitting there talking and watching the sunset, and that's when he kissed me."

"A sunset. A kiss. A definite prelude to sex," Merideth concluded knowingly.

"A kiss is a prelude to sex?" Sam rolled her eyes. "Maybe for you, it is."

Merideth arched a brow. "Oh, really? Seems as if I remember Nash winning you over in a similar way. A simple little kiss and you were panting after him for more."

"A simple little kiss?" Sam snorted a laugh. "Nash doesn't *do* simple little kisses. His are—"

"Okay, you two," Mandy lectured sternly, "knock it off. Alayna didn't come over to hear the details of your sordid sex lives." She turned back to her cousin. "He kissed you, then what happened?"

Alayna pressed her fingers against her lips, remembering her reaction. "It was horrible."

Merideth frowned, confused. "His kiss?"

Alayna frantically shook her head. "No, no. His kiss was wonderful. It was *after* the kiss that was horrible."

"What happened?"

"He—well, he put his hand on my breast, and I—" Alayna pressed a hand over her breast, remembering the feel of his hand there, then let it drop weakly to the table. "—well, I panicked."

Compassion softened Mandy's eyes as she reached for Alayna's hand. "Oh, Alayna."

Alayna blinked furiously, not wanting to cry, determined to say it all. "Then he left, and I was so embarrassed. I knew I shouldn't have let things go as far as they did. And I knew that I owed him an apology."

"You certainly did not!" Merideth cried, ready to come to her cousin's defense as quickly as she would that of her sisters. "A woman has to right to say no when she feels threatened."

Alayna lifted her gaze. "But I didn't want to say no. That's the problem." She squeezed her fingers tighter around Mandy's. "The next morning I tried to apologize to him, but then *he* apologized, insisting that it was all his fault."

Merideth smiled, pleased. "I might just grow to like this guy."

Alayna sighed heavily. "Then last night he asked me to stay with him." She wrinkled her nose and gave her head a shake, as she recalled the conversation. "Well, he didn't really *ask,* not in so many words."

"Did you?" Merideth prodded.

"Stay with him?" At Merideth's nod, Alayna sputtered a laugh. "Heavens, no!"

"Why?" This from Merideth again.

"Because it would have been a disaster! Just as it was when he kissed me."

"You don't know that for a fact."

"Oh, yes, I do," Alayna declared emphatically, then dropped her shoulders in frustration, frowning. "I was determined to go on as if nothing had happened, since we do have to work alongside each other every day. But then this morning, out of the blue, Jack became angry with me and asked me why I wore so many clothes."

All three McCloud sisters shared a look, having discussed the same thing themselves, though they all suspected they knew the answer.

"Then he took out his knife and cut the sleeve off of my shirt."

"He *what!*"

Alayna flapped a hand at Merideth to calm her ruffled feathers. "It wasn't like it sounds." She sighed again, releasing her grip on Mandy's hand. She sank back in her chair, her eyes going all dreamy as she replayed every detail of the event in her mind. "In fact, it was the most sensual experience I've ever had in my life."

Merideth and Sam looked at each other, their expressions saying, "Huh?"

"I wanted to grab him right then and there and make love with him. Or at least try to. But all I could think to say was 'Thank you.'"

Sam choked on a laugh and Mandy kicked her under the table. Sam kicked her back.

"Then, later," Alayna continued, unaware of the war being waged under the table, "he took me by the shoulders and looked me right in the eye and told me that I couldn't hide my sexuality any more than I could deny it."

Merideth shivered deliciously. "So then you made love with him. Right?"

"No." Alayna dropped her gaze, embarrassed. "I didn't know what to say, or what to do."

Merideth tossed her hands up in the air. "It's simple. You take him by the hand and lead him to your bedroom."

Alayna smiled wistfully, wagging her head. "Simple for you, maybe. But not for me. I'm no good at sex."

"Alex was an asshole, Alayna. Forget him."

For once, Mandy and Sam didn't correct Merideth. They, too, were aware of the emotional scars Alayna's ex had left her with.

"Our divorce was *not* Alex's fault," Alayna said firmly. "Not entirely, anyway," she added, frowning. "Granted, he wasn't the best husband in the world, but I can't fault him for my own inability to pleasure a man."

Sam squirmed uncomfortably in her chair. "Listen, Alayna, I didn't think I was cut out for sex, either, not after—well, not after what happened to me. But Nash proved me wrong."

Aware of the near rape Sam had suffered as a teenager, and the aversion to men that it had left her with, Alayna leaned to cover Sam's hand with hers. "And I'm happy for you, Sam. Nash is a wonderful man."

And Alayna was missing the point entirely. When she attempted to withdraw her hand, Sam tightened her fingers around it. "You're a psychologist, right?"

Alayna laughed uneasily at the intensity in Sam's gaze. "You know I am." She gave her hand a tug, but Sam refused to let her go.

"And as a psychologist," Sam persisted, "you know all about the different kinds of phobias and how to get people over them, right?"

"Well, yes, but—"

Sam tightened her fingers on Alayna's. "So what do you tell a patient who has a phobia? How do you get them over it?"

"I don't see the relevance..." Alayna began, glancing at her other two cousins in a silent plea for help. But both Mandy and Merideth just looked at her expectantly, waiting for her answer, as well. With a sigh, Alayna turned her gaze back to Sam's. "Well, the first step in the healing process is to get the patient to admit that the phobia exists."

Sam nodded. "Then what?"

"Then you develop a plan, working closely with the patient. Small steps where the patient can meet with success and thus gather the courage to proceed toward their ultimate goal."

"And your goal is to have sex with Jack, right?"

Alayna released a long, shuddery breath. "W-well, yes, I suppose. That's my initial goal."

"Does he want to have sex with you?"

Alayna thought about that a moment, then nodded slowly. "Yes, I think so."

Sam released Alayna's hand and flopped back in her chair, smiling proudly. "Problem solved. I'll send you a bill."

Doubts swarmed in Alayna's head. "But how? I've already refused his advances twice. How do I let him know that I've changed my mind?"

"You seduce him."

Merideth said it so easily, that Alayna had to laugh. "Seduce him," she repeated, then laughed again. She glanced down at her dress and caught a fistful of the long skirt and lifted it. "I don't think Jack finds me particularly seductive."

Merideth popped to her feet. "Wardrobe is my department and seduction my specialty." She held out a hand and gold bracelets clinked musically on her wrist. "Come with me, Alayna."

"Don't do it, Alayna!" Sam cried, rising, too. "She'll have you looking like a streetwalker."

Merideth stopped and slowly turned to face Sam, her lips pursed, her eyes narrowed dangerously. "I beg your pardon?"

Mandy quickly stepped between her two sisters. "Just keep it simple, Merideth," she suggested helpfully, giving her sister's arm a soothing pat. "Nothing too drastic."

Seven

Alayna stood before her bathroom mirror, frantically trying to style her hair. She was running late, which was a rarity, but this morning it had seemed to take forever to get the kids off to school. She suspected that it was her own impatience that had made the time pass so slowly. But the children were gone now, she reminded herself, and she had the house to herself.

Well, almost. Earlier, she'd heard Jack moving around downstairs, which meant she needed to hurry.

Drawing in a deep breath for courage, she set aside her hairbrush and smoothed her damp palms down her thighs. She turned to peer over her shoulder at her rear view and felt a flutter of nerves...even a little bit risqué.

Merideth had found the old pair of jeans Alayna now wore in Mandy's closet and had whacked off the legs, making them into shorts. She'd done the same to an old tank top, cropping the length to just beneath Alayna's breasts.

All in all the results were satisfactory, if a little frightening. Alayna couldn't remember the last time she'd worn a pair of shorts. Alex had always told her that she didn't have the figure to wear shorts, that her legs were too long, her thighs too fat. And she didn't remember ever wearing such a revealing top!

Were the shorts too short? she fretted. She gave the raveled hem a tug, trying to stretch the fabric, but quickly gave up. They'd just have to do.

She turned and adjusted the top, making sure it covered her bra, then lifted her gaze, meeting her reflection again. Could she really wear such a skimpy outfit in front of Jack? she asked herself. Would he think she was advertising? She pressed her fingers against her lips, stifling the hysterical giggle that bubbled up in her throat.

Oh, God, she hoped so!

She spun and all but ran for the stairs, anxious to test her new outfit—as well as the level of her nerves—on the unsuspecting Jack.

She found him in the kitchen already at work hanging a plate rack she'd discovered in the attic on the breakfast nook's newly stained wood wall.

At the sight of him, her heart stopped, then kicked into a frantic beat—and her bravado flew straight out the open window. She darted to the refrigerator and pulled open the door to hide behind it. "What would you like for breakfast this morning?"

His back to her, Jack tested the shelf by pressing a wide hand against its top, making sure it was sturdy. "Whatever. I'm not particular."

"It's so hot, how about just some fruit and muffins?"

Jack slipped the hammer into the loop on his tool belt.

"Sounds good to me." He turned, wiping his hands on a rag, just as Alayna pushed the refrigerator door shut with her hip. His eyebrows shot up as he got his first look at her and he blurted out the first thing that popped into his head. "You've got legs."

Her hands full, Alayna ducked and danced across the kitchen and to the counter, trying her best to make her shorts look longer and to hide her bare midriff. "I've always had legs. You've just never seen them." She set the fruit and muffins down, then stretched to her toes to pull plates from the cabinet. "I decided you were right. It's too hot to wear so many clothes."

Had he said that? Yeah, he had, Jack remembered, then cursed himself for making the suggestion. He'd never considered what the effect of a lesser-garbed Alayna would have on his system—as if it wasn't already in overdrive! He let out a slow breath as he watched her slip a hand behind her to give the hem of her shorts a discreet tug...and realized she was embarrassed. And he wasn't helping her a bit with his thoughtless comments.

And this was the very opportunity he needed to put his new plan into action. He would compliment her, build up her self-confidence and never have to lay a hand on her.

For some reason that plan had sounded a whole lot easier to implement when he'd been alone in the barn devising it. But, of course, then Alayna hadn't been prissing around in front of him half dressed.

He cleared his throat and had to force his gaze away from the lacy edge of panty that was peeking from beneath her shorts. "Well, you look...nice, Alayna. Real nice." *Nice?* He gave himself a mental thump on the head. Was that the best he could do?

She glanced over her shoulder and smiled shyly. "Thanks, Jack."

"You're welcome." He cleared his throat again. "What can I do to help?"

She turned and handed him a plate. "Nothing." She smiled again, this one a little easier, and a little more sure. "Just eat."

Jack took the plate and followed her to the table, not at all certain he could get anything past the sudden lump in his throat. "I thought I'd work on that bathroom upstairs this morning," he said, looking everywhere but at her. "You know. The one where the shower is leaking."

She sank gracefully onto a chair, setting her plate carefully in front of her and spreading a napkin across her lap. Without the baggy pants, her legs looked to Jack to be about a mile long. And, yeah, he did lose the battle of trying not to gape.

"That's fine," she replied.

He sat, too, dropping his plate onto the table in front of him. With both of them sitting now, his view of her was limited to her breasts and up. It should've helped.

But it didn't.

"If we get done early enough," he said, trying to keep his mind focused on the work he'd planned for the day, "I thought we might tackle the fireplace."

She bit into a strawberry, her eyes brightening as her gaze met his across the table. "Really?" Juice from the strawberry ran down her chin and she caught it with the tip of her finger, and scooped it up, then popped her finger into her mouth, sucking the juice from it. "What can I do to help?"

You can slide that sweet face of yours over here and let me lick that strawberry juice off your chin.

The thought formed before Jack could stop it. Thankfully, he caught himself before voicing it out loud. He tore his gaze from hers and hitched his chair closer to the table. He needed to take this slow, he reminded himself, and nonphysical. No telling what would happen if he were to touch her. All that bare skin...

Grabbing his knife, he slathered butter over his muffin, trying not to think about all that bare skin. "I don't know," he mumbled, focusing on his bread. "But I'll think of something."

"Hold it steady."

Alayna tightened her grip on the pipe but couldn't quit staring at Jack's bare back. He sat inside the old-fashioned footed bathtub, his shoulders hunched over his knees while he worked on the plumbing. Alayna stood outside the tub, all but salivating.

He'd stripped off his shirt again, and sweat beaded his skin and ran down his spine, soaking the waist of his faded jeans a darker blue. She swallowed hard as her gaze slipped to the band of white cotton at the small of his back where his jeans gapped open a bit. Boxers. He wore boxers. And, in Alayna's opinion, there was nothing sexier than a man wearing nothing but boxer shorts.

She remembered Tom Cruise in the movie *Risky Business* when he'd slid across a waxed floor, strumming an imaginary guitar and wearing nothing but a pair of white socks, white boxers and an unbuttoned white tailored shirt. She sighed lustily. What she'd give to see Jack similarly dressed.

"Hand me that wrench."

Startled, Alayna jumped, then quickly reached behind Jack, to retrieve the requested tool from the floor of the tub behind him. Her breasts brushed his shoulder as she leaned over him, and bolts of lightning arced through her body. Gulping, she straightened, and hastily passed him the wrench. Their fingers tangled in the exchange.

When she would have released her grip on the wrench, his hand closed over hers, holding hers in place. She glanced down and found him looking up at her. His eyes burned a hole straight through to her soul. She stood there staring, unable to move, unable to breathe while his thumb stroked across her knuckles. Once. Twice. On the third stroke, her knees buckled and she sank to the edge of the tub.

To his credit, Jack had tried to keep a safe distance and so busy that he wouldn't have a chance to think about how Alayna was dressed. But that one touch of her fingers against his skin had burned away all his good intentions. And when she'd sank to the edge of the tub...well, he was just plain lost.

Slowly he pried the wrench from her paralyzed fingers and tossed it to the floor before capturing her hand completely with his. One tug and he had her stretched across his lap, her legs dangling over the side of the footed tub.

With a groan, he covered her mouth with his.

Somehow, Alayna found the strength to lift her arms and wind them around his neck.

"Strawberries," he murmured, nipping at her lips. "I love strawberries."

Alayna mentally made a note to purchase more on her next visit to town.

He sipped her lips, then traced their shape with his tongue, as if savoring the flavor. "Damn, but I've been wanting to do that all morning," he said with a sigh, nuzzling her nose.

Wide-eyed, Alayna leaned back to stare. "Really?"

At the disbelief he saw in her eyes, Jack nodded his head. "Yeah, really."

He shifted his gaze to her chest and, unable to resist, smoothed a hand over her breast. He watched as her nipple budded beneath the thin knit fabric. He swallowed hard, digging deep for a control that was quickly slipping away from him. Compliments, he reminded himself. He needed to offer her compliments. "Did I tell you I like your shirt?"

Alayna shook her head, her breast aching for more of his touch. "No," she whispered. "You didn't."

He lifted his gaze to hers and saw the wonder in her eyes, as well as the heat. "Well, I do." He skimmed a hand around to her back and down to her hips, cupping a denim covered cheek in his palm. "I like your shorts, too."

"You do?"

He let a finger slide beneath the ragged hem and along the elastic edge of her panties. "Yeah. I do." He watched her eyes smolder, felt the tremble of nerves beneath her skin. "I like a lot about you."

"What?" she asked, seemingly mesmerized as much by his words as by his touch.

"I like the way you smile, the way your eyes light up when you're excited about something. And I like the way you walk, your hips sort of rolling from side to side, your hair swishing across your shoulder blades." He let his hand trail down the back of her thigh. "And I like the peeks I used to get every once in a long while of this soft skin here behind your knees." He stroked her there and her breath shuddered out of her. He stroked lower, moving his wide palm over her calf and around her ankle until it came to rest on her foot. "And I like your feet. They're so dainty and small, just like the rest of you." He slipped off one sandal, then the other, and let them drop to the floor. Cupping his palm around her arch, he drew her leg up, bending her knee and tipping her foot toward his face. He nipped her toe with his teeth then soothed the spot with his lips.

A shiver chased down Alayna's spine. "Oh, my heavens," she whispered breathlessly.

"Ticklish?" he asked, glancing her way.

"Yes. No." She closed her eyes in frustration. "I don't know."

He chuckled, guiding her leg back to the edge of the tub. "But you know what I like best?"

Her eyes flipped open to meet his. "What?"

"Your mouth." He dipped his head over hers and pressed a kiss to first her upper lip, then her lower one. "And your eyes," he added softly, lifting his head and looking deeply into them. "They are so blue. I remember thinking the first time I saw you that a man could drown in them."

"The afternoon in the café," she remembered.

"Yeah." He shifted, settling his back on the tub's sloped end and her more comfortably across his lap. "I thought you were an angel. You looked so beautiful, so innocent." His brow gathered in a frown as he rubbed the ball of his thumb across her lower lip. "Yet, so damn sexy."

It's simple. You take him by the hand and lead him to your bedroom.

Alayna heard Merideth's directive as clearly as if her cousin was standing over them, giving stage instructions.

But Alayna's bedroom was downstairs and she and Jack were upstairs sitting in the tub. If she suggested they go there, then she'd have to get up. Then he'd have to get up. Then they'd have to walk down the stairs and through the house. A lot could happen in that span of time. The spell could be broken. She could lose her nerve.

To hell with the bedroom, she thought, carelessly tossing aside Merideth's suggestion. The tub would do just fine.

"Do you know what I like about you?" she asked, trying to hide the quiver in her voice.

"What?"

"Your chest." She forced herself to lay her hand against it, and felt the thud of his heart beneath her palm. "It's so broad and muscular. I can't tell you how many times I've wished I could curl up against it like I did that night in the cabin."

"There's nothing stopping you from doing so now," he reminded her.

She looked up at him and he gave her a nod of encouragement. She smiled a bit nervously, then slowly threaded her fingers through the mat of hair there, watching her fingers' movement.

"Some women prefer a man without hair on his chest."

Alayna snapped her gaze to his. "Oh, no! I like a man with hair on his chest." To prove it, she laid her head against his chest and rubbed her cheek across it. "It feels so much softer than I thought it would."

In the movement, her cheek chafed his nipple and Jack flinched, sucking in a breath.

She quickly sat up and turned her face away, feeling the tears building. "I'm sorry. I didn't mean to—"

Jack placed a finger beneath her chin and forced her gaze to his. "You didn't do anything wrong, Alayna." He let his hand drop to her breast. "A man's nipples are sensitive like a woman's." He stroked once, and felt the shiver that shuddered through her. "See? Your body responds in the same way."

She didn't agree or deny his claim, but he could still see the uncertainties in her eyes. "It's okay, Alayna. You can touch me. You can do anything you want to me, whatever feels natural." When she still didn't move, he drew her hand to his chest and forced her palm open beneath his. He felt the tremble in her fingers and had to swallow the emotion that rose to his throat. "Talk to me. Tell me what's going on in that pretty head of yours."

"I—" She cleared her throat and tried again. "I'm afraid I'll do something wrong. That I won't please you."

"Just having you touch me is a pleasure." He wrapped an arm at her waist and drew her down until she was stretched along his length and they were lying stomach-to-stomach, nose-to-nose. "Now," he said, offering her a soft smile, "you were saying something about how the hair on my chest was softer than you thought it would be."

Alayna drew in a deep breath, silently praying that she wouldn't screw this up. "Yes," she replied, releasing the breath slowly. "I thought it would feel coarse. You know, rough."

"Disappointed?"

She took another deep breath. "No-o-o," she said slowly and shifted so that she could place her hand on his chest again. She laughed self-consciously. "In fact, every time you take off your shirt when we're working together, I have to will myself not to look."

"Why?"

She shifted again, and her leg slipped between his thighs. "Too tempting."

Jack was finding it harder and harder to breathe. And it wasn't Alayna's weight that was constricting his lungs.

"And you know what?" she asked him, finding her courage once again.

"What?"

She bit back a smile. "I love white boxer shorts."

Jack drew back his head to peer at her. "How'd you know I wear white boxer shorts?"

She smiled, pleased to discover that she could shock him. She pressed a nail into the hollow of his throat and began to trace a line down the middle of his chest. "I peeked." She rolled to her side, her back snug against the tub's wall, and let her finger trace lower. Her finger dipped into his navel, rose, then bumped to a stop against the waist of his jeans. She hesitated a moment, then forced her fingers to close around the top button of his jeans, releasing it. "Did you ever see the movie, *Risky Business?*"

"I—I'm not sure." He wasn't even sure of his name, anymore.

"Tom Cruise starred in it, and there is this scene where he slides across the floor in a pair of white socks, his shirt open and he's wearing nothing beneath it but a pair of white boxers." She released another button. "I rented that movie once, and nearly wore out the tape, replaying that scene over and over again." Another button popped open at her fingers' urging. "There's something about a man who wears boxers."

Taking a deep breath to strengthen her nerve, she slipped her hand into the opening she'd created and boldly took him into her hand. Her fingers shook slightly, but it didn't prevent her from feeling the softness of his flesh, the hardness of his arousal. Nor the heat. Slowly she lifted her gaze to his and found that same heat in his eyes.

And she, Alayna McCloud, had put it there.

Emboldened even more by that knowledge, she leaned closer. "Something *really* sexy," she added in a whisper and closed her mouth over his.

Jack couldn't think, couldn't move. He could only feel. And the woman pressed against him felt damn good. He hadn't intended to let things go this far, but he was helpless to put an end to it now. He framed her face with his hands, bringing her face closer, drawing her deeper into the kiss. He probed her mouth with his tongue, savoring her flavor, her taste, teasing her until she all but squirmed.

Her hand tightened around him and began to move slowly up and down his length...and he knew he was lost. He had to have her, had to make love to her, had to prove to her that she was capable of pleasing a man.

He dropped his hands to her shoulders and squeezed, marveling at the delicacy of her bone structure, the little whimper that escaped her as she pressed closer against him. Anxious to touch her, to show her what her body was capable of responding to, he slipped a hand underneath her short top and cupped a breast.

She gasped, her fingers vising around him.

"Easy," he murmured, pressing kisses to her chin, her throat, her chest. He felt her melt, muscle by slow muscle as he soothed her with his lips. Nudging her shirt's fabric down with his chin, he closed his mouth over a lace-covered breast. She arched against him, moaning softly. He smiled against her breast, then released it, replacing his lips with his hand.

"There's something else I like about you," he whispered at her ear, as he found the front hook of her bra.

"What?"

"Your breasts." He tugged her shirt up and over her head, and her hands went immediately to her chest, covering her nakedness.

He lifted his gaze to hers. "What are you doing?"

Her cheeks, already flushed with passion, reddened even more. "They're so small," she murmured almost apologetically.

He pushed her hands out of the way and looked, slipping her bra's straps over her shoulders and down her arms. He cupped her breasts in his hands as if measuring them. "They're perfect."

For some insane reason, Alayna believed him. Maybe it was the tone of his voice. Or perhaps it was the reverence with which he stroked her breasts. Or maybe it was the tenderness with which he pressed light kisses there, his breath warm and moist on her bare skin. Or maybe it was the sensations that spilled through her when he took her fully into his mouth and gently suckled. But suddenly she didn't feel lacking. She felt...almost whole.

"Jack?"

"Hmm."

"Make love to me."

Slowly he lifted his head and looked at her, his brown eyes searching hers. "Are you sure?"

She quickly nodded her head. "Yes," she whispered. "I'm sure."

Before he could respond, she sat up and began to pull his jeans and boxers over his hips. With his help, she freed him of them, then tossed them over the side of the tub. Struggling in the cramped space, she stripped off her shorts and lace panties, her hands shaking from a combination of nerves and anticipation. She dropped them on top of Jack's jeans, then moved to straddle him, her gaze on his.

"I want this, Jack," she whispered almost desperately as she reached between her legs to guide him to her. "I—"

"Alayna. Wait." He closed his hand over her wrist, stopping her. "I'm not protected."

She leaned closer, pressing her mouth over his as she lowered herself over him. "It's okay," she whispered huskily. "I can't have children."

Jack heard her, but was unsure what she meant. Then the words lost their importance as the softness of her feminine opening met the hardness of his arousal. "Alayna," he groaned, raising his hips to meet her.

She arched, sucking in a breath, as he slipped inside her, then groaned, her velvet walls closing around him instinctively. He grabbed her hips, holding her still, knowing if she moved so much as a millimeter, he'd lose his seed right then and there. And he wanted this to last more than he wanted to draw his next breath.

He waited, his fingers digging into her flesh, until he felt her slowly begin to relax. Then he began to move. In and out, setting the rhythm, raising his hips, then lowering them, guiding her with his hands at the curve of her waist, until she followed him, her movements as free and as spontaneous as the smiles she'd offered to him so many times over the last weeks.

Capturing her hand, he drew it to his chest, to his heart. "Do you feel that?" he asked, and pressed his palm flat over hers. Even through her hand he could feel the wild pounding of his heart and knew, though she said nothing, that she must feel it, too. "That's what you do to me," he whispered. "And this," he added and raised his hips, burying himself deeply inside her and allowing her to feel the fullness of his arousal. She gasped, then purred her pleasure, curling her fingers beneath his and digging her nails into his skin. "You make me want what I have no right to want," he told her, his voice husky with need. "To wish for things that I have no right to wish. You're a woman, Alayna, in every sense of the word. A very seductive woman.''

Tears misted her eyes. ''Oh, Jack...''

With his gaze fixed on hers, he began to move again, slowly at first, teasing her, then filling her, drawing her closer and closer to a fire that burned within them both. Passion stained her cheeks, glazed her eyes, while perspiration beaded her upper lip and dampened the hair at her temples. Jack watched her face, and knew that she was close. Suddenly she cried out, then tensed, as if straining to grasp something held just out of her reach.

''Let go, Alayna.'' he whispered, watching her. ''Let me set you free.''

He thrust hard, bringing her hips to meet his and she cried out again, arching against him as she accepted his seed. She filled her hands with her hair, stretching her arms up high, then higher still, letting the long blond strands drift through her fingers and fall to pool at her shoulders.

Then she crumpled, melting against his chest on a thready sigh, her heart echoing the pulsations of her feminine walls around him. He gathered her within his arms, holding her close to him, and pressed his lips to the top of her head.

Cradled within the old-fashioned footed tub, he closed his eyes and rested his cheek against her angel-blond hair.

Slowly a sense of peace slipped over him.

Eight

The sense of peace Jack experienced after making love with Alayna lasted about as long as the nap they took together in the tub.

The phone rang, startling them awake.

Alayna bolted upright, her hip digging painfully into Jack's groin. She glanced around, disoriented for a moment, before her gaze settled on Jack's. As she brought him into focus, a slow smile of remembrance curved her lips and warmed her eyes. She melted to his chest and covered his mouth with hers.

And the phone rang again.

She withdrew reluctantly, replacing her lips with a finger and pressed lightly. "Hold that thought," she whispered.

She quickly scrambled from the tub and grabbed the portable phone from the back of the toilet tank where it rested.

"Hello?"

Her eyes widened and she grabbed Jack's shirt from the toilet seat and frantically stuffed her arms through the sleeves as if whoever was on the other end of the line could see her nakedness. "No! No!" she cried. "You didn't interrupt anything." She glanced Jack's way and rolled her eyes, then brushed her hair back from her face and held it on top of her head while she listened. Her eyes grew even wider.

"Yes. I've got plenty of room." She fisted her fingers in her hair and pulled it up away from her head, then released it, letting out a silent whoop of joy. "Yes, I'll be here this afternoon. No problem." She spun in a tight circle, hugging the phone to her ear. "Yes, and thank you. Thank you so much."

Jack watched as she carefully hit the disconnect button and replaced the phone on top of the toilet's tank. Then she whirled. "A baby!" she squealed shrilly. "They're bringing us a baby!"

She dived over the side of the tub, planting an exuberant kiss on Jack's lips, then, just as quickly, she was pushing against his chest and popping back to her feet. "Oh, my stars!" she cried, clapping her hands over her cheeks. "I've got so much to do!" She grabbed her shorts and tugged them on, and began reciting a list. "I've got to get the crib down from the attic. Launder the crib linens and receiving blankets. I've got to sterilize the bottles—"

She disappeared through the bathroom doorway, still ticking off her list of things to do…and left Jack sitting in the tub, naked as the day he was born, staring after her.

* * *

All Alayna could think about was that a baby was being delivered to her home that afternoon.

All Jack could think about was that Alayna had said she couldn't have any children.

She couldn't have kids.

He laid the shelf across the brackets he'd hung on the wall of the room Alayna had chosen for the nursery and slapped his level on top.

She couldn't have kids?

What the hell was that supposed to mean? he asked himself in frustration. Was she on some type of birth control? Or had she meant that she *physically* couldn't have children? He watched the level's bubble rock a moment before it finally settled over the center point. He snatched the level from the shelf and stuffed it into the pocket of the nail apron he had tied around his waist.

Didn't matter, he told himself. The fact was she wanted children. And Jack didn't. Not his. And not anyone else's.

He glanced toward the opposite side of the room where Alayna knelt, putting together the frame of the crib. Her hair was still mussed from their lovemaking, and she was still wearing his shirt. He found it hard to believe that they'd made love less than an hour ago. And it hadn't been just sex, either. They'd made wild passionate love, something Alayna had thought herself incapable of.

The fact that he'd proven to her that she could please a man should have made him feel good, since that was the gift he'd wanted to give her. But for some reason he felt bluer than blue.

At that moment she glanced up and caught him looking at her. A slow knowing smile curved at her mouth and turned her eyes to smoke. "What are you looking at?"

Jack lifted a shoulder and crossed to her. "Just admiring your shirt."

He took the wrench from her and tightened the bolt, accomplishing in two seconds what Alayna had failed to do in ten minutes. She laughed, rocking back on her hips and wrapping her arms around her knees. "Want it back?" she teased.

Jack glanced at her and was tempted to strip the shirt from her, pull her into his arms and make wild passionate love to her right there on the nursery room floor.

Instead he snorted and tossed the wrench into the toolbox. "You've got a stork delivery due this afternoon, remember?" He pressed his hands against his thighs and pushed himself to his feet. He stood over her, his hands braced against his hips. "So what's next on your list, boss lady? Laundering the sheets, or sterilizing baby bottles?"

Jack stood at the second floor nursery window with his arms folded across his chest, watching the circus on the lawn below. It seemed a delivery from the stork was a family affair for the McCloud family. All three of Alayna's cousins had been called to witness the event. He'd recognized Sam and Mandy right off when they had driven up, and he figured the woman who had just arrived driving a sporty Porsche must be their sister, Merideth.

He whistled low under his breath when he saw the car door open and a long, curvy leg appear. He let his gaze travel up the leg and to the face of the woman as she stood, pushing back a mane of blond hair. Seemed beauty ran deep in the McCloud bloodline, he reflected. Every single one of the McCloud women was a looker.

Then it hit him. Merideth McCloud. The movie actress. He hadn't made the association until he'd gotten a full view of her face. And what a face! In person, she was even more beautiful than she appeared on the theater screen.

He watched a smile spread across her face, then she was racing across the lawn and toward Alayna. When she reached her, she threw an arm around Alayna's shoulder and pressed her cheek close to hers as she looked down at the baby. Two beautiful faces. Two beautiful women. But in Jack's estimation, Merideth didn't hold a candle to Alayna's beauty.

"I don't know why they're making such a fuss. It's just a stupid baby."

Jack glanced down, unaware that Billy had slipped into the room and was standing beside him. The boy stood with his arms folded across his chest, his posture the mirror image of Jack's. Jack recognized the resentfulness in the boy's stance, and slowly forced his own arms to his sides. He turned his face back to the window.

"You don't like babies?"

Billy snorted. "All's they do is cry, burp and pee."

Jack bit back a smile. "You were a baby once," he reminded the boy.

Billy folded his arms more stubbornly across his chest. "Yeah, but nobody made all that fuss over me. Not that I'd want 'em to," he added quickly.

Jack glanced down and saw the thrust of the boy's lower lip, the resentfulness in his stance. "You don't like hugs and kisses?" he asked.

"Heck, no! Kissin' and huggin' is for sissies."

Jack lifted his shoulder and turned his gaze back to the window. "Personally I kind of like hugs and kisses."

Billy snapped his head up to look at Jack. "You do?" he asked doubtfully.

Jack nodded. "Sure do."

Billy turned his head back to stare out the window. "Alayna gives me hugs and kisses sometimes," he admitted reluctantly. "I guess hers are all right." He frowned. "But she'll forget all about us now that the stupid baby's here."

Jack heard the bitterness in the boy's voice. But he heard the fear, too. "I'm sure she'll be busy with the baby, but she won't forget you're here. Molly, either. She'll probably even need your help."

"I ain't changin' no stinkin' diapers."

Jack chuckled. "I doubt she'll ask for your help with that chore." He turned his gaze back to the window, folding his arms across his chest again.

He felt a slight pressure against his side as Billy eased closer. They stood there together, looking down below and watching as the baby was passed from one expectant set of arms to another. Gradually the weight of Billy's body against Jack's side increased.

Jack suspected that the boy was feeling left out, and was worried about his place in the order of things now that there was a baby in the house. The hell of it was, Jack was feeling much the same emotions.

"Have you ever done any carpentry work?" he asked offhandedly.

Billy looked up at Jack, then snorted as he turned his face back to the window, scowling. "I'm just a kid. Remember?"

Jack lifted a shoulder. "Never too young to learn."

Billy glanced back up, his eyes narrowed suspiciously. "Learn what?"

"A trade. I could use some help around here. Of course, you'd have to be pretty strong for the work I'm needing done."

Billy bent his arm at the elbow and pushed up a sleeve,

showing his muscle. "I've got big muscles," he said proudly.

Jack curled his fingers around the small swell on the boy's arm and tried to hide a smile. "Yep. That's pretty big all right. Think you could swing a hammer?"

"Shoot, yeah," Billy bragged.

Jack gave Billy a slap on his back that aimed him toward the door. "Well, let's get to it, then, before somebody comes looking for us and wants us to change a diaper."

"Here?"

Jack nodded as he knelt beside Billy, holding the lattice panel in place. "Yep. That's the spot. Just give the nail a tap to set it in the wood."

Billy lifted the hammer and thumped it against the nail. When he released the nail, it fell to the ground. He turned to Jack, scowling.

Jack chuckled and picked up the nail, passing it back to Billy. "Try it again. Only this time, hit it a little harder."

With a sigh of frustration, Billy put the nail back into position. Narrowing his eyes in determination, he lifted the hammer and swung. It hit the wood, missing the nail entirely.

"Again," Jack instructed patiently.

Billy swung again, harder this time. Slowly he released his grip on the nail. He grinned when it stayed in place.

"Perfect," Jack said. "Now you can drive it into the wood, but be careful that you don't bend the nail."

Catching his lower lip between his teeth, Billy lifted the hammer with both hands and pounded it against the nail. He missed the nail a couple of times, and hit the wood instead, putting a few dents in it. But Jack figured a few dents in the wood didn't matter. Billy was busy and he was happy, and he didn't seem to be fretting over the baby any longer, which was what Jack had hoped for when he'd suggested that Billy help him with his work.

Billy rocked back on his heels and looked up at Jack. "Is that good enough?" he asked uncertainly.

Jack shot him a grin. "Couldn't have done it any better myself."

His chest swelled with pride, Billy stood. He stuck the end of the hammer into his jean pocket, trying to use his pocket in the same way that Jack used the loops on his tool belt. Unfortunately his pocket wasn't deep enough and the hammer fell to the ground dangerously close to Billy's feet.

"Guess we're going to have to get you a tool belt," Jack said as he stooped to pick up the hammer.

Billy's eyes widened in excitement. "Really? When?"

Jack slipped the hammer into the loop on his own tool belt. "Next time I'm in town."

"Cool, dude!"

Chuckling, Jack playfully ruffled the boy's hair. "Yeah, cool."

Jack heard the cries before he even reached the house.

Man, that kid's got a set of lungs!

He opened the back door and stepped inside the kitchen. Alayna stood at the stove, stirring something in a pan while she jounced the screaming baby on her shoulder. Her hair was mussed and she was wearing the same blue robe Jack had seen her in that first morning when he'd come to the Pond House to work.

At the sound of the door closing, she turned and offered him a tired smile. "Good morning."

Jack tossed his cap to the counter. "Good morning."

She turned back to the stove and continued her stirring, raising her voice to be heard over the baby. "We're having oatmeal. I hope that's all right."

"Oatmeal's fine," he said, raising his voice, as well.

He watched her whack the spoon against the side of the pan, then lay it aside. The baby screamed even louder. Alayna sighed wearily and patted the infant on the back as she crossed to the refrigerator for milk. Jack noticed the droop of Alayna's shoulders, the heaviness of her step, the shadows beneath her eyes. He quickly gathered bowls and utensils and crossed to the table.

"Did you get any sleep last night?" he asked.

Alayna smiled weakly as she set the milk on the table, then sank wearily into a chair. "No," she said, dipping her head to look at the baby. "Meggie cried all night."

"Is she sick or something?"

Alayna lifted her head to look at him and he saw the circles beneath her eyes, and the tears that brightened them. "Mrs. Lindstrom, the social worker," she added in explanation and sniffed, "says she has colic. I gave her the medicine they left with me, but it didn't seem to help."

Jack wasn't sure what possessed him, but he found himself rounding the table and holding out his hands. "Here. I'll take her for a while."

Alayna sighed gratefully as they made the exchange, wiping the stray tear from her cheek. "Thanks, Jack." She pushed herself to her feet. "Just give me a minute to get the oatmeal, then I'll take her back." She shuffled her way to the stove, retrieved the pan of oatmeal, then shuffled her way back to the table as if her feet were weighted with lead. She yawned hugely, then covered her mouth with her hand when she saw Jack watching her. "Sorry," she murmured in apology.

"I'd say you're due."

He watched as she scooped oatmeal into their bowls as if the spoon alone weighed a hundred pounds, then shuffled her way to the sink where she deposited the empty pan. She turned, holding out her arms as she crossed back to him. "Here. I can take her now."

Jack shifted the baby to his left shoulder and away from Alayna. "She can scream in my ear as easily as she can scream in yours." He gestured for her to take her seat. "Go on and eat your breakfast."

Alayna hesitated only a moment, then moved to her chair. She sank down onto it, propped her elbow on the table and her cheek on her palm. She sprinkled sugar over her oatmeal. "I had no idea a baby could cry this long."

"She's got a set of lungs on her, that's for sure."

Alayna tried to smile, but decided it required too much effort. She stirred oatmeal around her bowl, too exhausted to even lift the spoon and take a bite. She watched Jack as he shoveled spoonfuls of oatmeal into his mouth while alternately patting the baby's back.

"You're pretty good at that," she said, surprised by the ease with which he handled the baby.

With his spoon halfway to his mouth, Jack froze. He forced himself to carry the spoon the rest of the way, slowly chewed the food, then swallowed. "What's so hard about holding a baby?"

Alayna shrugged. "Nothing, I guess, though I've rarely seen a man hold an infant with such ease, especially a crying one."

Jack laid aside his spoon and shifted the baby to his lap, stretching her out across his thighs. He rubbed his hand over her back, throwing in a pat now and again.

After a moment, the baby burped, hitched a shuddery breath, then grew quiet.

Alayna's eyes widened as she stared at the baby. "How did you do that?"

Jack watched the movement of his hand across the infant's narrow back and remembered another time he'd handled a baby in such a way.

"My son had colic," he said in a voice so low Alayna had to strain to hear it.

Her gaze snapped to his. "You have a son?" she asked in surprise.

"*Had,*" he corrected. "I lost him a little over six months ago in a car wreck."

Alayna sank back against her chair, slowly absorbing the news. Jack had lost a son. That explained so much. The lack of emotion in his eyes. His avoidance of Billy and Molly. "Oh, Jack," she murmured sadly. "I'm so sorry."

He rose quickly, shifting the baby to his arms, then rounded the table and held the infant out to Alayna, avoiding her gaze. "I better get to work." After making the exchange, he turned and headed for the door.

Alayna pressed the diaper tab into place, then pulled the soft pink kimono down over Meggie's skinny legs. "All dry," she said, smiling as she lifted the baby into her arms. Meggie seemed more content now that she'd received the second dose of colic medicine—at least, she wasn't crying any longer.

Humming softly, Alayna walked to the window and looked out across the lawn and toward the old barn. Two sawhorses were sitting in the barn's open doorway and the Pond House's front door lay stretched across their tops. Jack stood beside the sawhorses, stooped, his hands braced against an electric sander, a long black cord stretched out behind him. Chips of old paint flew from beneath the sander while a thin cloud of dust puffed around his head. She watched as he paused to smooth a hand across the wood, testing its surface, then put the sander back in place. A sigh shuddered through her.

She remembered the feel of those same hands smoothing across her bare skin. Wide, strong, rough with calluses, yet gentle. Oh, so gentle.

Slowly she turned away from the window and moved to sit down in the rocker. Shifting Meggie to cradle the infant in her arms, she pressed her foot to the carpet and set the rocker into motion.

He had a son. Jack had a son.

It explained so much, she thought as she rocked slowly to and fro. The emptiness in his eyes, the lack of emotion there. His avoidance of Billy and Molly. And it explained the question he'd asked her that night in the cabin.

How do you do it? How do you let them go?

She realized now that he'd asked the question out of personal need, not out of curiosity. It seemed that Jack was having a hard time dealing with the loss of his son and handling the grief associated with that loss.

She felt a kick against her stomach and focused once again on the baby she held. Meggie stared up at her, her blue eyes wide and unblinking. Smiling softly, Alayna touched a finger to the corner of the baby's mouth. Meggie turned her face at the touch, her mouth opening and seeking as if she were a baby bird waiting for her mommy bird to drop in a worm.

"And where are your mommy and daddy?" Alayna asked Meggie. With a regretful shake of her head, she reached for the bottle she'd left on the changing table and tickled Meggie's lips with its nipple. Meggie opened her mouth and began to suck greedily.

Alayna rocked slowly, staring down at the baby, her

mind warring against all the injustices in the world. Lives lost in senseless tragedies. People with the ability to produce children like rabbits, but who didn't want the burden of a child, while others, who would trade anything for the gift of a child, were left childless.

Why? she cried silently. Oh, God, why?

There was no answer to her question, but then Alayna had expected none.

But she did recognize a similarity in her and Jack's lives. Jack had had a child, and lost him. Alayna had never had a child, but felt the same loss. Jack had lost a part of his heart on a highway somewhere. Alayna had lost a part of hers in a doctor's sterile office with the words, ''You're barren.''

Yet, she saw differences in their situations, as well. Alayna had discovered a way to share her love with a child, while Jack had closed his heart from feeling anything.

That's not true, she thought with a shake of her head, though it had been true when Jack had first arrived. But he had changed over the weeks he'd been with them. She'd seen the emotion that had darkened his eyes when he'd returned Molly's bear to her and Molly had kissed him. And she'd watched the way he interacted with Billy, a child he claimed to dislike, offering guidance to the boy with an equal measure of patience and care.

Oddly Alayna felt no need to meddle, or to offer the wisdom of her education to help Jack deal with his grief. The children—Billy, Molly, and even Meggie, she reflected, glancing down at the sleeping face of the infant she held—were doing a very good job of that on their own.

Jack braced a hand on the door, holding it in place while Billy aligned the pin above the hinge. ''Just give the pin a slight tap to set it in place.''

Billy lifted the hammer and thumped it against the metal pin's head, sinking it about a quarter of the way down into the hinge's slot. "Like that?" he asked, looking up at Jack for approval.

"Looks good to me. Now give it a few solid whacks, but be careful not to dent the pin's head.''

Firming his lips in determination, Billy lifted the hammer and pounded it against the pin, setting it deeply in place. He braced the hammer against the floor of the porch and looked up at Jack again. "How's that?''

Jack shot him a grin. "Good job." He held out his hand and Billy passed him the hammer. Jack took another pin, and held it in place above the door's highest hinge. He lifted the hammer and drove the pin into the slot in one smooth swing.

"Wow," Billy murmured, impressed. "You only had to hit it once. It took me 'bout four swings.''

Jack laughed and ruffled the boy's hair. "Yeah, but I'm bigger than you and I've had more practice.''

Laughing, Billy ducked from beneath Jack's hand and skipped down the steps at Jack's side. "What's next?" he asked. "Are we gonna hammer something else?''

"Nope. I thought we might try your hand at painting.''

Billy raced ahead a few steps, then turned, jogging backward. "Cool, dude! I know how to paint. We paint all the time at school.''

Jack laughed, thinking that the job he had in mind for Billy might be on a larger scale than the painting the boy had done in the classroom. "Good. Then you won't need much instruction.''

Billy continued to jog backward, his arms pumping. "What're we gonna paint?''

"The gazebo."

Billy stumbled to a stop. "The gazebo?" he repeated. "The one by the pond?"

Jack stopped, too, frowning. "Yeah. You got a problem with that?"

Billy stole a glance at the house, then looked back at Jack and grinned. "Nope. Race you!" he challenged and took off at a run for the barn.

Jack hesitated only a second, then loped after him. He caught up with Billy quickly, scooped the boy up underneath his arm and raced on.

Billy squealed, laughing as he bounced roughly against Jack's side.

Nine

"It sure is hot."

Jack wiped the excess paint from his brush, then nodded his head as he straightened to stand before one of the gazebo's support columns. "Yep, it is," he replied.

"I'll bet the water's cool, though."

Jack glanced over at Billy. The boy was standing, staring wistfully at the pond, his paintbrush hanging uselessly at his side, dripping paint onto the grass. Jack bit back a smile. "Yeah, I'll bet it is. You can take a break, if you want to. You're due one."

Billy whipped his head around, his eyes wide with excitement. "I can go swimming?"

"Can you swim?"

Billy grinned. "Sure I can!"

Jack gave him a nod. "Fine with me, then. Strip down to your drawers, so you'll have some dry clothes to put on when you're done."

Before the instructions were even out of Jack's mouth, Billy had dropped to the ground and was shucking off his shoes and socks. He hopped back to his feet, peeling his shirt over his head. He gave his jeans a shove over his hips and kicked free of them, leaving him wearing nothing but a pair of Scooby Doo briefs. Jack shook his head, laughing as Billy raced for the pier.

Billy and those jeans of his, Jack thought, still chuckling. They were so big the kid didn't even have to bother with unbuttoning or unzipping them. He just gave them a shove and they dropped to the ground.

"Hey, Jack! Watch this!"

Billy stood at the end of the pier, waving wildly. Jack grinned and returned the wave. Taking a deep breath, the boy pinched his nose between thumb and finger and jumped in. Water splashed a good four feet in the air when the kid hit the surface in the worst belly flop of a dive Jack had ever seen.

Jack winced, feeling the sting on his own flesh, then shook his head, smiling wistfully. He remembered a time when he and his twin brother Travis used to have contests to see who could make the highest splash. Of course, Travis had always won. Of the two of them, Travis was the most athletic, the most daring. He could swim like a fish, hunt like a hound and had nerves of steel.

Jack frowned as he thought about his brother, wondering how Travis was managing alone, running the building business they owned in partnership. Jack shook off the guilt that rose, and focused his gaze on the pond, watching the ripples smooth, the water's surface turn to glass once again.

The boy ought to be coming up for air by now, he thought, and took a step toward the shore. He took another step, then he was running, stripping his shirt over his head. He ran down the pier, the boards pitching wildly beneath his feet. Keeping his eyes glued to the spot where Billy had jumped in, he kicked off his boots, took a deep breath and dived in.

Water burned through his nose as he plunged beneath the surface. He kicked hard, driving himself deeper, his arms pushing against the weight of the water and searching. Squinting his eyes against the murky water, he spun slowly, looking for some sign of Billy.

His lungs screamed for oxygen, and Jack knew that he had to find Billy soon. Time was running out.

He felt something brush the back of his calves, and he whipped himself around.

Billy!

He grabbed the lifeless boy hard against his chest and kicked furiously for the surface, swimming with one hand and holding Billy tight against him with the other. He broke through the surface, gasping for air. He quickly rolled Billy to his back and his face to the sky. The boy's eyes were closed, his mouth slack, his skin a deathly white. Pond water dribbled from his mouth.

Swallowing back the fear that rose, Jack wrapped an arm around the boy and swam for the pier, towing the boy along with him.

"Don't you dare die on me, Billy," he threatened, his voice raw. "Don't you dare die."

Jack sat beside the hospital bed, his shoulders hunched forward, his elbows on his thighs, his hands dangling between his knees. His gaze was fixed on the little boy who lay on the bed, a monitor bleeping a record of his vital signs while he slept.

Alayna wondered what was keeping Jack upright. He

had to be exhausted after sitting beside the bed all through the night. "Jack?" she called softly.

When he didn't respond, she tiptoed across the room and laid a hand on his shoulder. "Jack?"

He twisted around at her touch, brought her into focus and slowly rose. "Did you talk to the doctor?"

The sight of his ravaged face nearly brought Alayna to her knees. She pressed her fingers to her lips to still their trembling. "Y-yes. H-he's going to be all right," she said. "The scan showed no sign of brain damage."

Jack dropped his chin to his chest and heaved a breath of relief. "Thank God," he murmured.

"Jack," Alayna said, reaching out to touch his arm, "why don't you go home and get some rest. I'll stay with Billy."

Jack spun and sat back down, resuming his watch. "No. I'll stay."

"But, Jack—"

"No," he repeated more firmly. "I need to be here when he wakes up."

Alayna wanted to argue with him, insist that he go home and get some sleep, but she knew that she'd just be wasting her breath. Jack wasn't leaving Billy's side until the boy woke up and assured Jack himself that he was going to be all right. Jack blamed himself for the accident and nothing anyone could say or do would convince him otherwise.

Wanting to comfort him, to ease his guilt, she placed a hand on his shoulder. She felt the tension in him, felt the shudder that passed through him before he lifted his hand and covered hers with his own. The strength of his grip, the desperation in it, brought tears to her eyes.

"If anything had happened to him... If he had... I—"

But Alayna couldn't allow him to say the words she

knew he was going to say. She leaned over, and wrapped her arms around him from the back, pressing her cheek against his. "It wasn't your fault, Jack."

"I shouldn't have let him go near the water."

"But you didn't know that Billy couldn't swim."

"Still…"

Frustrated by his insistence on shouldering the burden of guilt alone, Alayna withdrew her arms from around him, and knelt on the floor at his side. Taking his hand in hers, she squeezed, forcing his gaze to hers. "This is about more than Billy isn't it, Jack?"

Sucking in a raw breath, he tore his gaze away from hers.

She squeezed tighter. "It is, isn't it, Jack? This is about your son."

He bolted to his feet, tearing his hand from her grasp. He stared down at her, his chest heaving. "Don't try digging around in my head, Doc. I told you before, you might not like what you find there."

Alayna rose, too. "Jack," she said softly, reaching for him.

He took a step back and away from her, lifting his hands high to avoid her touch. Then he turned and stalked to the window. Alayna stared at his stiff back, her heart breaking. She wanted so badly to help him, to comfort him. She dropped her chin to her chest. But how could she help him when he refused to talk to her, refused her offer of comfort?

"It was my week to have him."

At the sound of his voice, Alayna slowly lifted her head, afraid to move for fear that he would stop talking.

"He had just turned four and he and his mother were going out of town. I was supposed to drop him off at her house on Friday afternoon. On the way there, I got a page from my office. We were nearby, so I decided to just whip by the office and see what the problem was. Josh loved going to my office."

She could see Jack's reflection on the glass, and saw the soft smile that the memory of his son drew.

"He liked to sit at my drafting board and draw pictures. And he liked to build forts from the brick samples we kept on hand." He drew in a deep breath, and firmed his lips, leaning to brace his hands against the windowsill. "I had my secretary call Susie and tell her that I was going to be late. That really peeved Susie off. Within minutes she was storming into my office, screaming at me and telling me what a lousy father I was, what an even lousier husband I had been, and that this was a perfect example of how she couldn't rely on me for anything." He paused, his fingers tightening on the sill. "Josh started crying. He hated it when we fought. But his tears seemed to anger Susie even more. She grabbed him and tore out of my office." He pushed from the ledge and stood tall, folding his arms across his chest, his gaze narrowed on the glass. "That was the last time I saw my son alive. They were both killed in an accident less than an hour later."

"It wasn't your fault, Jack."

He grunted, but kept his gaze on the window. "Yeah, I know. At least I do here," he said, stabbing a finger viciously against his temple. "But my heart," he said his voice softening as he dropped his hand to massage at his chest, "tells me different. If I'd taken Josh to his mother's instead of stopping by the office, as I was supposed to, then maybe things would've turned out differently. Maybe they wouldn't have been on that stretch of road when the 18-wheeler lost control and hit them."

With all her education, with all her experience in dealing with people with emotional and psychological problems, people who had experienced grief as deeply as Jack had, Alayna should have been able to think of something to say to him. Something that would take away his guilt, or, at the very least, ease it.

But she could think of nothing. Nothing.

And she knew the reason why. She loved Jack. She didn't know when her feelings for him had deepened to that level, but they had. And because she loved him, she'd lost her objectivity, her ability to offer him anything other than her comfort.

And he didn't seem to want even that from her.

She moved to stand behind him and lifted her hand, wanting to touch him, to reassure him, to give him the solace of her heart. But he must have sensed her intent because he stiffened and shifted away.

"Go home, Alayna," he said, his gaze fixed on the window. "Molly needs you. And Meggie needs you. I'll stay with Billy. I give you my word that I'll keep him safe this time."

Alayna felt the tears rise. They burned her throat, stung her eyes. Slowly she turned away. At the door, she paused and looked back. *I love you, Jack,* she wanted to say. *We all do.*

"Jack?"

Jack jerked up his head, instantly awake. Billy lay in the bed opposite him, his eyes open and filled with fear. The monitor that had bleeped during the night was silent. Jack wondered when the nurse had turned it off, and felt guilty that he'd fallen asleep during his watch.

Jack rose quickly, and braced his hands on the side of the bed. "It's okay, champ," he said, his voice thick with emotion. When he saw the boy's lips tremble, he lifted a hand and combed the hair from the child's forehead. "You're going to be just fine. I promise."

Billy stared up at him, his eyes filled with tears. "Are y-you mad at me?"

His heart nearly breaking, Jack eased up on the bed beside Billy. Wrapping an arm around the boy's shoulders, he drew him to his side. "No, I'm not mad at you, son."

"But I lied. I told you I could swim and I couldn't."

Jack laughed weakly, relieved to see that Billy was all right, and that the kid was more concerned about the lie he'd told than he was about his close brush with death. "You sank like a rock."

Billy inched closer, pressing himself against Jack's side. "I know. And it was spooky. I kept trying to find my way back to the top, but it was dark. I guess I got lost."

Jack hugged the boy tighter against him. "Yeah, I guess you did. But you're going to be all right now."

The door opened with a soft *whoosh* and Billy and Jack both looked up. Alayna's head appeared in the doorway. Her gaze met Jack's and locked, then she forced her gaze on to Billy's. She smiled, her eyes filled with a mixture of tenderness and relief as she looked at him. "You're awake."

He rubbed a hand over his head, mussing his hair, embarrassed. "Yeah."

She opened the door wider. "I brought someone to see you."

She stepped to the side, revealing a very frightened Molly who stood in the opening holding her Teddy.

"It's okay, Molly," Billy said, with a wry grin. "I ain't dead or nothin'."

Molly tucked the bear under her arm and ran across

the room. At the side of the bed, she stopped and held up her bear. "You can keep Teddy so you won't be afraid."

Billy scowled, his face turning red. "I ain't scared." When he saw Molly's disappointment, he reached for the bear. "I'll keep him, though. Just in case."

Molly beamed a smile, then climbed up on the bed and parked herself beside Billy. "I'm not scared, neither," she said, leaning close to whisper in Billy's ear. "Not anymore."

Jack wasn't sure which it was—the gift of the bear, or Molly's admission that she wasn't afraid any more—but he suddenly felt a lump in his throat the size of a watermelon. He stole a glance at Alayna and saw that she was standing, staring at her makeshift family, her fingers pressed against her lips, tears glistening in her eyes. Obviously the little scene between Billy and Molly had moved her as much as it had Jack.

But Jack didn't belong in this scene. He wasn't a part of this family. He didn't want to be a part. He eased his arm from around Billy's shoulders and off the bed. "I guess I better head home. I've got work to do."

"Don't go, Jack!" Billy cried.

Jack set his jaw. "Alayna's here now. She'll stay with you." He turned quickly away, and dragged his cap from the bedside table. He jerked it on his head as he headed for the door. "Call if you need me," he said to Alayna as he passed by her.

Then he was gone.

Jack worked like a madman, completing one job only to race on to the next. He was a man with a mission...and his mission was to finish the remodeling job and get the hell off the Double-Cross Heart Ranch and as far down the road as he could get.

He never should have taken the job in the first place, he told himself as he laid tile on the newly remodeled bathroom floor. He should've just kept driving, chasing that white line, burning up miles while he tried to outrun his guilt, his grief.

He tore out the weathered boards that sealed off the fireplace, and cursed himself for being a fool.

He scraped chunks of dried caulk from around the windowpanes and prayed that he could finish the job before he lost his resolve.

He'd told himself that he wouldn't let them get to him—Alayna or her brood of kids—but somehow they'd managed to slip inside his heart when he wasn't looking.

He'd thought for sure he'd died in that car wreck with his son over six months before, or convinced, at least, that his heart had died. But he'd discovered that his heart was still beating. He could still feel pain. He still had the ability to care.

And he didn't want to care. He didn't want to hurt anymore.

And he didn't want to hurt anyone else.

At night, when he should've been sleeping, when the Pond House was dark and Alayna and the kids were safe in their beds, he'd slip out to the barn and work on the old harvest table. He'd give her that, he promised himself. He'd give Alayna the table that had seemed to mean so much to her.

But he couldn't give her any more than that.

He just didn't have it to give.

"He's leaving."

Mandy glanced from the baby she held to Alayna who

was standing at the sink, her arms hugged around her waist, staring out the kitchen window. "Who? Jack?"

Alayna nodded.

Mandy shifted Meggie to her shoulder and crossed to the sink to stand beside Alayna. She looked out the window and saw Jack tossing old lumber onto the bed of his truck. "Looks to me like he's working," Mandy said dryly, "not packing."

Alayna let her arms drop and turned away, unable to bear the pain of looking at him any longer. "That's just it. He works from dawn till dusk, without ever taking a break. He doesn't even come to the house for dinner anymore."

Mandy followed Alayna to the table and sat down beside her. "Has he said anything about leaving?"

Alayna picked up a plastic toy of Meggie's and slowly turned it in her hands. "No. But he wants to. I can sense it."

"He's a grown man, Alayna. If he wanted to leave, he'd leave."

Alayna wagged her head. "No. He gave me his word when I hired him that he'd stay until the remodeling job was finished." She glanced toward the window again, and caught her lower lip between her teeth. "That's why he's working so hard. He wants to finish. Jack would never go back on his word."

Merideth sailed into the room, fluttering her hands above her head. "Somebody else has to entertain Billy for a while," she said wearily and sagged down onto a chair. "I'm pooped."

Alayna forced a smile and pushed to her feet. "I will," she said, but Mandy stopped her with a hand on her arm.

"No, you will not." She rose, shifting the sleeping baby to her shoulder. "I'll pop in a video for Billy and put the baby down for her nap, then I'm coming right back down here and we are going to have a talk.'' She turned to Merideth. ''And you,'' she said, pointing a stern finger, ''are going to make a batch of margaritas. I think we're going to need one. Maybe two,'' she added as she headed for the stairs. ''And call Sam,'' she tossed over her shoulder. ''We may need her input.''

Jack opened the front door and slipped inside. He could hear voices coming from the kitchen, and assumed that all the women were still gathered in the kitchen. Kind of late for a gab session, he noted with a glance at the grandfather clock in the hall. It was after ten. Usually Alayna was in bed by this hour. With a shrug, he tightened his hand on the burlap sack he carried and headed for the stairs.

He had to hand it to them, though, he thought with a nod of approval. The McClouds stuck together. All three of Alayna's cousins had filled in for Alayna while Billy had been in the hospital. They'd taken Molly and Meggie home with them and shared the duties of caring for both girls during Alayna's absence from home. And after Billy's return from the hospital, they'd been on hand every day to help Alayna entertain him and to help her out in any way that they could. And when a boy with as much energy as Billy was confined to bed for a week...well, he required a lot of entertaining.

Jack reached the top of the stairs and turned for Billy's room, then stopped. He was leaving, but he couldn't leave without saying goodbye to all the kids.

He crossed to the first room, the nursery that he'd helped Alayna set up. He tiptoed across the room to the crib. Bending over, he laid a hand on Meggie's narrow back, feeling the rhythmic beat of her heart beneath his palm. He closed his eyes and inhaled deeply, filling his senses with the scent of baby powder and innocence, those sweet, sweet smells associated with an infant.

She shifted beneath his hand, and flopped her head over, turning her face to the opposite cheek. In the glow of the night-light, he stared at her profile. The bud of a nose. The puckered lips. The sweep of lashes against her cheek. The tiny shell of her ear. Leaning closer, he pressed a kiss to her cheek, then withdrew, placing a finger against the spot he'd kissed, as if to seal it.

"Goodbye, Meggie," he whispered. "Sweet dreams."

He dug a wooden doll from the sack and set it on the changing table, then left quickly and slipped into the next room. Molly was asleep on her side, her chin resting on the top of Teddy's head. He brushed a finger across the blond curls that feathered her cheek. Such a sweet face, he thought, staring at her. Such a brave little girl, he reflected, thinking of all the nights she'd stayed alone with no one but Teddy to keep her safe.

He remembered the night she'd sent Teddy to him, knowing what a sacrifice that had been for her. He remembered, too, the kiss she'd given him, the feel of her little body pressed against his legs when she'd wrapped her arms around his thighs and clung.

He leaned over and brushed a kiss on her cheek, then slowly withdrew, setting each feature to memory. "Be safe, Molly," he whispered. Reaching into the sack, he pulled out the high chair he'd made for Teddy and propped it on the floor beside the bed. He rubbed a finger beneath his nose as he stole one last look and told himself he wouldn't cry. He sniffed before he made a liar out of himself and turned for the hall.

In Billy's room, he paused and drew in a deep breath, knowing that this goodbye might well be the hardest. He crept to the bed, holding the sack in one hand and leaned over.

Billy popped up and they bumped heads.

"Jeez," Jack muttered, rubbing his sore forehead. "What have you got in there? Rocks?"

Billy stretched to turn on the bedside lamp, then flopped back against his pillow, grinning. "Nah. Just a lot of brains."

Jack chuckled and dropped down on the side of the bed, still rubbing his forehead. "Yeah, right." He cut a glance at Billy, frowning. "What are you doing awake at this hour?"

Billy shrugged. "I never sleep." At Jack's skeptical look, he added, "Well, not much." Seeing the sack, he crawled to Jack's side and plopped down on the edge of the bed beside him. "Whatcha got in there?" he asked, peering at the sack curiously.

Jack lifted the sack, then let it drop. "Just something I picked up in town."

"Something for me?" Billy asked, leaning farther over for a better look.

Jack caught him by the collar of his pajamas and hauled him back onto the bed before he fell to the floor. "Yeah, something for you."

"What is it?"

Jack handed him the sack. "See for yourself."

Billy opened the sack and stuck his head inside. "Oh, dude!" he whispered. "This is too cool." He pulled the sack from over his head and shoved a hand inside, fishing to the bottom of the sack. He withdrew the gift and held it up. "A tool belt," he said, staring at it in awe. "Is this really for me?" he asked, turning to look at Jack.

Not trusting his voice, Jack nodded.

"Cool!" Billy hopped up to stand on the mattress and

whipped the belt around his waist, bending his head over so he could see to fasten it in place. He lifted his head, and a grin split his face from ear to ear. "Thanks, Jack," he said, and held up his hand.

Jack slapped it with his own, then stood. "Now hop back into bed before Alayna catches you up and skins both our heads."

Billy dropped to his bottom, laughing as he bounced on the mattress. "She won't be mad," he said. "We made a deal. I can stay awake as late as I want just so long as I stay in my bed." He grinned impishly up at Jack. "And I'm *in* my bed."

Jack shook his head, chuckling, and reached to ruffle Billy's hair. "Well, I'm not, so I guess I'd be the one to get my head skinned." He pulled back the covers. "Now in you go," he ordered. Billy flopped down on his back and Jack pulled the sheet over his chest. He switched off the lamp and started to withdraw. Billy stopped him by calling his name.

"Jack?"

"Yeah?"

"Are you leavin' or something?"

Jack pressed his lips together and nodded. "Yeah, Billy. I'm leaving."

"Why?"

Jack lifted a shoulder. "My work here's all done."

"I'll bet Alayna'd let you stay if you asked."

Jack shook his head. "No. It's time I moved on."

"Will you come back and see us?"

Jack thought he heard tears in the boy's voice, but couldn't be sure. "I don't know, Billy."

Billy slipped down lower on his pillow, drawing the sheet to his chin. "Don't you like us?"

Jack had to suck in a deep breath before he could answer that one. "Yeah, Billy, I like you just fine. But—well, it's just time for me to move on." He bent over, lifting a hand to give Billy a high five. Billy lifted his hand, too, but before his hand touched Jack's, he jack-knifed from the bed and threw himself against Jack's chest. "I don't want you to go," he sobbed. "I want you to stay here with us."

Strangled by the tears that gathered in his throat, Jack hugged the boy tight against him, sure that his heart was going to break. Slowly, he peeled Billy's arms from around his neck. He guided him back beneath the covers and smoothed a hand across his forehead. "I wish I could, Billy," he whispered. "I wish I could."

He straightened, and took a step back. "Now you stay out of trouble, you hear me?"

"Yessir," Billy mumbled, then sniffed.

"And you take care of Alayna and the girls, all right?"

"I will."

"Bye, Billy," Jack whispered as he backed from the room.

"Bye, Jack," he heard the boy whisper in return.

Ten

Jack opened his eyes, instantly awake. Someone was in the cabin. He listened for another sound, wondering if he had time to grab the whiskey bottle beneath his bed to use as a weapon. He heard a soft footstep behind him, and cursed his habit of sleeping with his back to the door. He knew that if it came to a fight, he'd have to rely on his hands. There wouldn't be time to go for the bottle.

He felt the mattress dip behind him and he rolled to his side with a feral growl, his hand fisted and ready to throw a punch. He managed to stop his hand inches from a shadowed face that looked all too familiar.

"Alayna?"

She shrank away from him, eyeing the doubled-up fist inches from her nose. "Y-yes," she whispered, then laughed nervously. "It's me."

Jack dropped his fist to the mattress with a groan, then shot her a frown. "Don't you know it's not safe to sneak up on a sleeping man that way? I could've broken your nose.''

She pulled back the covers and slipped beneath them. ''But you didn't.''

There was just enough moonlight coming through the window that he could see her face. Not clearly, but enough to see that she was smiling.

''What in the hell do you think you're doing?'' he asked as she curled a foot around his bare leg.

Her smile drew nearer. ''I came to seduce you,'' she whispered and he would swear that was liquor he smelled on her breath.

''Seduce me,'' he repeated, staring at her as if she'd just grown two horns.

''Yes, seduce you.'' She snuggled closer, laying a hand on his bare thigh and stroking.

He jerked his leg back, knocking her hand away. ''Are you drunk?''

She laughed, sitting up to toss her hair back over her shoulder, then rested her cheek on her palm. ''I remember asking you that one time.''

Jack's frown deepened. ''Yeah, I remember that, too. But I wasn't drunk.''

''I'm not, either.''

He peered more closely at her, squinting to better see her face in the darkness. ''Are you sure?''

''Yes. I'm sure. I only had two margaritas.''

''Two margaritas,'' he repeated, then cocked his head to look at her suspiciously. ''Is that what you and your cousins were doing in the kitchen till all hours of the night? Drinking margaritas?''

She nodded her head. ''That and talking.''

He narrowed an eye at her. ''And where are your cousins now?''

"Well, Merideth and Mandy went home, but Sam stayed."

"She's at the house?"

"Yes."

"Why?"

"Because she drew the shortest straw."

Jack heaved a frustrated breath. "No. I mean, why is she still at the house?"

"Well, I couldn't very well leave the children in the house alone."

Jack suddenly felt as if a spotlight had been turned on his bed and he had an audience of three women waiting for his performance. He knew how women loved to talk. "And your cousins knew you were coming over here to seduce me?" He waited, praying he'd misunderstood her and dreading hearing her answer at the same time.

"Well, yes," she replied hesitantly. "It was their idea."

Jack groaned, and buried his face in his hands. It was worse than he'd thought.

Alayna sat up. "And what is wrong with their plan? I thought it was rather clever, myself."

He opened his hands enough to get a look at her face to make sure that she was serious. "Clever? You think *this* is clever?"

Alayna flipped back the covers and flounced from the bed. She whirled, hands on hips. "Yes, clever," she snapped peevishly. She tossed out a hand, gesturing toward the house. "With three innocent children in my house, I couldn't very well invite you to spend the night with me. And I couldn't leave them alone, either." She folded her arms beneath her breasts. "This seemed the perfect solution."

Jack wished now that she had stayed in the bed, then

maybe he wouldn't have noticed that she was wearing that blue robe of hers. The one that matched her eyes. And he wouldn't have gotten that peek of her breasts, either, when she'd flung out her arm, pointing toward the house. But with her standing right in front of the window with moonlight spilling over her form, he saw it all.

He covered his face with his hands again, groaning, then scraped his fingers up over his face and back through his hair. "The perfect solution for what?" he asked, striving for patience.

Tears flooded her eyes. "I wanted to make love with you again before you left, and I couldn't think of a way—"

Jack held up a hand, interrupting her. "Before I left? You knew I was leaving?"

She nodded.

Jack sighed, dropping his hand to the mattress, and his gaze there, as well. He rubbed the ball of his thumb across the cotton sheet. "I was going to tell you in the morning."

"You don't owe me an explanation. I—"

Jack held up his hand again, but this time he motioned her toward the bed.

Though she did so with reluctance, Alayna moved to the side of the bed. Jack stretched across the width of mattress that separated them and took her hand, drawing her down beside him. "Yes, I do," he said, wearily, staring at their joined hands. "I should have told you before now, but—well, I couldn't." He lifted his gaze to hers. "I have to go, Alayna. It's time for me to move on."

She nodded, tears clotting her throat. "I—I know."

Jack wagged his head. "No, I don't think you do." He inhaled deeply, searching for the words. "I didn't want to care," he said slowly. "I thought I could just do my job without getting involved. But I couldn't." He firmed his lips and glanced back over his shoulder to the window and the house beyond. "Billy and Molly and then Meggie." He wagged his head again, then turned to stare at their hands. He laced his fingers through hers, unlaced them, then laced them again. Finally he lifted his head, squeezing her fingers between his. "It hurts, Alayna. And I don't want to hurt anymore."

Tears streaming down her cheeks, Alayna leaned over, smoothing a hand tenderly across his cheek. "I know, Jack. And I understand. I really do."

He raised a hand and closed it over hers, holding her palm against his cheek. "And it's just not the kids. I—well, I care for you, too."

A sob hitched in her chest and she unwound her fingers from his to press them against her lips.

"You deserve a man who can be a part of a family and I can't do that, Alayna. I wish I could, but I can't. I don't want any more children."

She moved her hand from her lips to his. "Shh," she whispered. "Don't say anything more." She moved her hands to frame his face. "I want to make love with you, Jack," she whispered. "One last time."

Searching his eyes, she drew closer, pressing her lips lightly against his. "Will you, Jack?" she asked, her breath warm and moist against his. "Will you make love with me?"

Jack drew her down beside him, matching her length to his. "Yes," he whispered, kicking the sheet from his legs. "God help me, but yes," he groaned and covered her mouth with his.

Alayna almost wept at the feel of his mouth on hers. The taste, the texture, the hunger with which he seemed to devour her. And when his hand found her breast, she sighed, giving herself over to the sensations he drew. She closed her eyes, determined to remember every detail. The width of his hand, the strength in it. Each and every callus that chafed against her bare skin.

And his lips when he suckled her. Gently at first, then drawing her more fully into his mouth, his tongue laving her nipple until she ached for more.

And more never seemed to be enough.

She framed his face with her hands, feeling the muscles of his jaw work, glorying in the sensations that flooded her body. He lifted his head to meet her gaze, then used his weight to push her onto her back, never once taking his eyes from hers.

He spoke not with words, but with his hands and with his eyes, telling her how precious she was to him. And Alayna knew his feelings, saw them in his eyes, felt them in every stroke of his fingers across her flesh. Never had she felt more loved than she had at that moment, never so blessed.

Kneeling beside her, he opened her robe fully, then sank back on his heels, moving his gaze to hers. "You are so beautiful," he whispered, laying a palm on her stomach. "So very, very beautiful." He leaned and pressed a kiss to her abdomen, then lifted his head to look at her. "I wish I could put a baby here," he whispered. "One of your very own for you to love."

Alayna felt the familiar tears swell, but this time there was no regret, no sense of inadequacy because she didn't have the ability to produce the child he wanted to gift her with. There was only a sense of joy that Jack cared enough to want to give her her dreams.

Reaching for him, she drew his face to hers and sighed her pleasure against his lips as he moved over her, matching his body to her length. She spread her legs, creating a nest for him, welcoming him in…then gasped when the heat of his arousal touched her feminine opening. She arched to meet him, taking him in, then followed him in a dance that had existed since the beginning of time.

She stroked his back with her hands, shaping each straining muscle, then moved her hands to his chest, seeking the beat of his heart, the warmth of his soul.

And when he dropped his chest against hers, she wrapped her arms around his neck and clung while he whispered in her ear, "Come with me, Alayna. Come with me now."

She closed her eyes and focused on his movements, feeling each ebb and flow of his body within her. The heat built to a blinding inferno and she knotted her fingers in his hair. She pressed her head back against the pillow, unable to bear the sensations that seemed to keep building and building within her, demanding release, and Jack pressed his lips to the smooth column of her throat. "Now," he growled against her fevered skin. "Now!" And he drove himself deeply inside her.

Alayna heard a guttural cry and was shocked when she realized that it was her own. Then she was falling, falling, faster and faster until her head spun with the dizzying sensation and her body felt as if it was no longer her own.

The explosion came simultaneously, a shower of blinding light that left her breathless and weak. She reached for Jack, certain that she had lost him in the fall, and felt a shudder rack his body. Then he collapsed, letting his full weight rest on her and she welcomed the pressure, wrapping her arms around his neck and holding him close.

She rubbed her cheek against his, loving the feel of his beard scraping her skin, then turned her lips to his ear. "I love you, Jack," she whispered. "I love you so much."

When he tensed, she clutched him tighter to her. "It's okay," she reassured him. "You don't have to love me, too."

Slowly Jack relaxed, grateful for her understanding. He rolled to his side, drawing her with him and molding her shape to his. He dipped his head to look into her eyes. What he found there filled him with peace. No condemnation, no regrets, just clear blue eyes that met his gaze openly and without a hint of remorse. He smiled softly, then tucked her head in the curve of his neck. With a sigh, he pressed his lips to the top of her head, then rested his chin there.

"Sleep with me, Alayna," he whispered and closed his eyes.

Jack awakened before dawn and rolled over, instinctively reaching for Alayna, as if he had done so every morning of his life.

But his hands found only cool sheets. He opened his eyes, then closed them with a groan when he confirmed that she wasn't there. He fisted his hands against the soft cotton. She was gone.

And soon he would be, too.

Jack checked the fastening on his camper that he had replaced over his truck's bed the night before, made sure it was secure, then headed for the driver's side of his truck. He opened the door, then paused, hooking an arm through the open window as he looked one last time in the direction of the house. Setting his jaw, he climbed into his truck and started the engine.

He shifted into drive and pressed down on the accelerator, and focused on the road ahead. He passed by the house and pushed his foot a little closer to the floorboard. By the time he reached the highway, he was all but flying.

Or was that running?

He shook his head and set his eyes on the white line marking the center of the highway. He'd chase the white line, he told himself, and see where it took him. And he wouldn't look back.

He didn't dare.

Alayna stepped onto the patio, and looked up at the morning sky. She closed her eyes and hugged her arms beneath her breasts, drawing in a deep breath. It's going to be a wonderful day, she promised herself.

Releasing the breath, she opened her eyes and looked out across the pond to the hills where the sun was showing off its morning colors.

He was gone. She knew without looking toward the cabin, or the barn, that Jack had already left. She sensed the loss before she turned and verified that his truck was missing.

She drew in a shuddery breath and pressed her hand against her heart. She wouldn't be sad, she told herself. He had left her with nothing but wonderful memories.

She turned for the house, and stumbled to a stop, her hand going again to her heart. There beside the back door stood the old harvest table, its oak patina glowing radiantly in the morning sun. Pressing her fingers against her lips, she crossed to it and laid a hand on the polished wood. She could almost feel the care that had gone into restoring it. The warmth of Jack's hand. The tenderness with which he had worked on the scarred wood.

She smoothed her hand across the top, unashamed of

the tears that dripped onto the surface and beaded there. He'd done this for her, she thought, feeling her heart swell, because he'd understood how much the old table had meant to her.

She couldn't help but wonder what she had meant to him.

Jack drove until his eyes burned and the register on the gas gauge was drifting on the wrong side of empty. Seeing a service station ahead, he whipped onto the asphalt deck and stopped beside the pump.

Climbing out of his truck, he pressed his hands to his back and stretched. He kicked out a leg as he rounded the hood, getting the blood flowing again. He'd been driving for a good five hours.

He slipped a credit card into the slot, punched in his selection, then pulled the nozzle from its anchor. Whistling to pass the time, he stuck the nozzle into his gas tank, and squeezed the lever. He turned his back to his truck, propped a foot against the tire while the gas pumped and looked around. The station was like a hundred others he'd stopped at during the six months he'd been on the run.

And now he was on the run again.

He ducked his head and fitted his thumb and finger over his eyes and rubbed. He wouldn't think about them, he told himself. He'd—

He jumped when he felt the truck rock against his back and turned to stare at it. He waited to see if it moved again. If it didn't, he was afraid he was losing his mind.

He almost laughed at that. Hell, he'd lost his mind a long time ago. That, and his heart.

But then he thought he caught a slight movement. Shutting off the gas, he shoved the nozzle back into its anchor, then moved quietly to the back of his truck. He stared at the camper door a moment, wondering what waited for him on the other side.

Frowning, he twisted the handle and jerked the door wide.

Billy sat on the floor of the camper, his eyes bugged wide. He gulped, then tried a shaky grin. "Hi, Jack."

Jack braced his hands on his hips. "What in the hell do you think you're doing?"

Billy crawled to the door and swung his legs over and dropped to the ground. He looked up at Jack, squinting against the sun. "Running away with you."

Jack grabbed him by the arm and marched him a few feet away, then spun him around. "Does Alayna know where you are?"

"No, sir."

"Do you have any idea how worried she must be right now?"

Billy ducked his head and chipped at the rough asphalt driveway with the toe of his tennis shoe. "I guess she'd be pretty worried."

"Well, I'm taking you back," Jack said angrily as he tugged the boy by the elbow and dragged him toward a phone booth. "But first we're going to call her and tell her you are all right."

Billy dug in his heels, dragging Jack to a stop. "No, please, Jack," he begged. "Don't take me back. I want to go with you."

Jack braced his hands on his hips, glaring down at the boy. "You're not going with me, all right? You're going back to Alayna's." He whirled and marched on. "Now come on. We're going to call her."

Billy ran to catch up with him, pulling on the back of his shirt to stop him. "No, Jack, please. I don't want to go back there. I want to go with you." When Jack turned to glare at him again, Billy's eyes were filled with tears. "I won't be any trouble. I promise. And I can work for you, just like I did when we were at Alayna's. I'll work hard. You'll see. And I won't eat much, so you don't have to worry about buying me a bunch of food. Please, Jack?"

Jack inhaled deeply, and slowly dropped to a knee. "Billy, you have a home with Alayna. I don't have a home for you."

"I don't need a home. I can sleep in the camper with you. There's room."

"Alayna will miss you, Billy."

He ducked his head. "No, she won't. Not for long, anyways. Nobody wants me. My mom and dad didn't. And those other foster people didn't, either. They just keep me for a while then move me on to another house. Nobody cares what happens to me."

Jack watched a tear fall and splat against the asphalt. Setting his jaw, he stretched out an arm and yanked Billy hard against his chest and to his knee. "I care, Billy," he said, his voice gruff with emotion. "And Alayna does, too."

"Then t-take me with you, J-Jack. *Ple-e-ease?*"

Jack let his head fall back as pain ripped through his chest. How could he turn his back on this boy who needed him? How many more parts of his heart could he afford to leave behind before there was nothing left? How could he bear to say goodbye to the kid one more time? How far would he have to run before he realized that he couldn't outrun his grief? It always seemed to be there waiting for him, when he stopped to catch his breath.

And how could he leave Alayna? How could he survive even a day without the beauty of her smile, the comfort and warmth of her touch? He needed her. He wanted her. He loved her.

Setting his jaw, Jack gathered Billy up in his arms and carried him to the truck. He opened the door and sat Billy down on the passenger seat and strapped the seat belt around him. Billy watched him through tear-filled eyes. "What're you doin? Where're you goin', Jack?" he asked when Jack started to close the door.

Jack paused, then reached inside and cupped his hand over Billy's head. "I'm going to call Alayna and tell her that we're coming home."

"*We?*" Billy echoed. "You mean you're going home, too?"

Jack blew out a long breath. "If Alayna will let me stay."

Billy let out a whoop, kicking his feet up in the air. "She'll let you stay, Jack! I just know she will."

Alayna paced in front of the window, casting nervous glances out the window. "They should be here by now," she said with a nervous glance at the grandfather clock.

"You know how kids are," Mandy soothed. "Jack probably had to stop every couple of miles to feed Billy or let him use the restroom."

Alayna choked on a laugh. "No, I *don't* know how kids are, but I'm learning. The hard way." She pressed her hands against her temples. "Oh, Mandy. What if Billy doesn't want to stay with me any longer? How will I ever be able to let him go?"

Mandy wrapped her arms around Alayna and hugged her. "That's the hell of being a parent," she said with a sigh. "We never know how long we'll have to hold on to them." She planted her hands on Alayna's shoulders and dipped her head to meet her cousin's gaze. "Look at Jack. He had a son and lost him way before he was ready to let go. My Jaime is almost seventeen and he's already kicking at the chute wanting Jesse and me to let him run free." She sighed again. "And I'm not ready to let him go.

"I don't know that I'll *ever* be ready. It's a mother's curse," she said wrapping an arm around Alayna's shoulder and walking with her to the door. "We work so hard to teach our children to be independent, then we cry when they leave us and strike out on their own." She shook her head, then pulled Alayna closer to her side. "Just love him while you have him," she told her. "That's the best a mother can do."

Mandy pushed open the screen door. "Jaime! Jesse! Load those kids into the truck and let's head home."

Jaime waved and scooped Molly from the swing and onto his back, giving her a piggyback ride. Jesse followed at a slower pace, holding his Stetson over Meggie to shield her face from the low-hanging sun.

Mandy smiled as she watched her husband and son. "But all the headaches and heartaches are worth it," she added, then turned and offered Alayna a reassuring smile. "You'll see."

Alayna heard the sound of a truck and raced to the window, shoving back the drape to press her nose against the glass. Twin dots of light bounced toward her through the darkness, growing larger by the second. With her heart in her throat, she opened the front door and stepped out onto the porch just as Jack braked to a stop and switched off the headlights. He opened his door, stepped to the ground and closed it behind him. He paused, turning to look at her. She lifted a hand, and he did the same.

She tried her best to get a good look at his face, to read his expression.

Before she could, he turned away and rounded the hood, moving to the passenger door. He opened it, and ducked inside. Moments later, he reappeared, carrying Billy in his arms.

Alayna raced down the steps to meet him. "Is he hurt?" she asked, laying a hand on Billy's bent knee.

"No. Asleep. I think he probably stayed up all night waiting for an opportunity to sneak out to the camper and hide."

Alayna stepped back, giving Jack room to pass. "Thank heavens," she murmured with relief, then ran to open the front door for him.

She followed him up the stairs to Billy's room, and helped him strip off the boy's clothes and tuck him into bed. Once they'd accomplished the task, they stood side by side, both staring down at the sleeping boy, their arms folded across their chests as if afraid that they might accidentally touch each other if they let them dangle free.

Alayna leaned a shoulder against Jack's, lifting her hand from her forearm to squeeze his. "Thanks for bringing him home," she whispered. "I was so worried."

Jack dropped his arms and placed a hand against the small of her back, giving her a nudge toward the door. "I imagine you were."

They walked down the stairs together, and Alayna was at a loss as to what to say. Everything in her told her to grab ahold of Jack and beg him to stay but she realized how unfair that would be to him. She had to be strong for his sake.

At the foot of the stairs, she forced a smile, knowing that dragging out the goodbye would only make it worse for both of them. "I really appreciate your bringing Billy home."

Jack stopped and pulled off his cap, crushing it between his hands. "It was no trouble." He cleared his throat, and dropped his gaze to his hat. Slowly he smoothed the creases from it. "Alayna, you said something to me last night that I haven't been able to get off my mind."

She cocked her head, looking at him in puzzlement. "What?"

"You said that you loved me."

Alayna felt the heat crawl up her neck and stain her cheeks. "Yes, I did. I mean, I do." She huffed a breath, stiffening her arms at her sides. "What I mean to say, is that, yes, I love you, but that places you under no obligation to love me in return."

Jack looked up at her. "I wasn't finished yet," he said, trying not to smile.

"Oh." She pressed a hand to her throat in embarrassment, then waved it at him. "Well, go on, then. What was it that I said that has been troubling you?"

"You said that I didn't have to say it back."

Alayna looked at him, confused. "Well, that's exactly what I meant to say. You *don't* have to say it back. A person can have feelings for another person without that person having to return those same feelings."

Jack shook his head as if to clear it. "Is that a bunch of that psychological mumbo jumbo you picked up in that fancy school you went to back east?"

"What?"

"That 'this person and that person' stuff? Because if it is, you're gonna have to say it in plain English if you want me to understand."

Alayna pursed her lips. "What it means, in *layman's*

terms," she added pointedly, "is this. I can love you without you feeling obligated to love me back."

"But I do."

"Well, fine, then. Now why don't we—" She stopped, her eyes going wide. "You *what?*"

"I do."

"You do, what?"

"I do love you."

Alayna could only stare. "You do?"

Jack gave his chin a jerk. "Yeah, I do."

She slipped a hand to cover her mouth, and the other to clutch her stomach.

"You're not going to get sick, are you?" Jack asked, peering at her closely. "'Cause if you are, I'll run and fetch you a basin or something to throw up in."

Alayna sputtered a laugh that sounded more like a sob, and waved her hand in front of her face to stem the tears that threatened. "No, I'm not going to get sick. I'm just—I'm just surprised, is all. Oh, Jack, I—"

But then she was in his arms and his mouth was on hers, stealing her words as well as her breath. "Alayna, Alayna, Alayna," he murmured, rocking her from side to side as he absorbed her warmth and the feel of her. "I don't want to run anymore."

She caught his face between her hands and held him there. "You don't have to, Jack. You're home now."

He closed his eyes and leaned to press his forehead against hers, wanting to believe that it was that easy. "But I'm scared, Alayna. Scared I'll screw this up somehow." He drew back to meet her gaze. "I want to marry you, and be a father to Billy, and Molly and Meggie, but I'm scared that I'll disappoint you, that I'll let you all down somehow."

Alayna pressed her hands against his cheeks. "But you

will disappoint me, Jack. And I'll disappoint you, too. As well as the children. That's just part of life. But our love for each other is what will carry us over the rough spots.''

Jack groaned and pulled her into his arms, burying his nose in her hair. "I do love you, Alayna. I love you so much it hurts.''

"And I love you," she whispered, hugging him close.

He drew back again, cupping her shoulders within his hands. He dipped his knees, looking deeply into her eyes. "I want to have a baby. Us," he clarified. "I want us to have a baby. One of our own.''

He watched the blood drain from her face and wondered what he'd said to make her react that way.

"I can't have children, Jack. I told you that.''

"But I thought you meant—never mind," he said, and pulled her into his arms again. But this time her arms didn't come up to wrap around him and hug him back.

And Jack knew he'd said the wrong thing.

Slowly he stepped back, sliding his hands down her arms to capture her hands. "It doesn't matter, Alayna.''

"Yes, it does," she said, dropping her chin. "If not now, it will later. You're young and healthy. You could have more children if you wanted to.''

Jack released one of her hands to push a knuckle beneath her chin, forcing her gaze to his. "No, it doesn't matter," he said softly. "Not now, and not later. I've got you, and that's all I'll ever want or need. But if you want to fill this house with kids, then that's fine with me. I'll love them, too. And if you want to adopt some of those kids, that's okay, too. We'll provide for them all the best we can.''

Unable to bear the misery in her eyes, Jack pulled her into his arms again, rubbing his hand up and down her back, willing her to believe him, to trust that he'd never renege on his promise. "I only said I wanted us to have a baby of our own because I thought that was what you wanted," he explained. "Truly, Alayna, I'm satisfied with exactly what we've got. I give you my word on that."

Slowly he felt the resistance ease from her body. Slower still, he felt her arms lift to wrap around his waist. Then she was hugging him with a fierceness that nearly stole his breath.

"And you never go back on your word, do you, Jack?" she said, drawing back far enough to look at him.

"No, ma'am, I don't," he said. "My word's as good as any legal document you could have drawn up."

"And I have your word that I can fill this house up with children?"

"Yes, ma'am," he said, beginning to smile. "As many as you want."

"And we can adopt some of them, too, if we're offered the opportunity?"

"Yes, ma'am," he said, laughing. "As many as you want."

"Then let's get married."

"That's a damn good idea."

"For better or worse," she said, pressing a finger against his lips and looking deeply into his eyes, "I'm yours."

"And I'm yours," he returned, and swung her up in his arms.

"Can I be the first kid you adopt?"

Jack froze and he and Alayna both looked up to find Billy sitting at the top of the stairs, his legs swinging from between the banister spools.

"That depends," Jack said, narrowing an eye at the boy.

"On what?" Billy asked.

"On how fast you can get back to bed."

Billy was on his feet and running before Jack could blink his eyes.

"I'm fast," Billy yelled over his shoulder. "Really, really, fast."

Jack chuckled and shifted Alayna in his arms, searching for a better grip. He jerked his head in the direction of the stairs. "Are you sure you want a houseful of kids like him?"

"Yes," she said laughing. "Just like Billy."

* * * * *

Look for Peggy Moreland's next book in October 1999, BILLIONAIRE BRIDEGROOM, an emotional and fun story that's part of THE TEXAS CATTLEMAN'S CLUB, only from Silhouette Desire. And look for another TEXAS BRIDES from Peggy in 2000!

If you enjoyed what you just read,
then we've got an offer you can't resist!

Take 2 bestselling love stories FREE!

Plus get a FREE surprise gift!

Clip this page and mail it to Silhouette Reader Service™

IN U.S.A.
3010 Walden Ave.
P.O. Box 1867
Buffalo, N.Y. 14240-1867

IN CANADA
P.O. Box 609
Fort Erie, Ontario
L2A 5X3

YES! Please send me 2 free Silhouette Desire® novels and my free surprise gift. Then send me 6 brand-new novels every month, which I will receive months before they're available in stores. In the U.S.A., bill me at the bargain price of $3.12 plus 25¢ delivery per book and applicable sales tax, if any*. In Canada, bill me at the bargain price of $3.49 plus 25¢ delivery per book and applicable taxes**. That's the complete price and a savings of over 10% off the cover prices—what a great deal! I understand that accepting the 2 free books and gift places me under no obligation ever to buy any books. I can always return a shipment and cancel at any time. Even if I never buy another book from Silhouette, the 2 free books and gift are mine to keep forever. So why not take us up on our invitation. You'll be glad you did!

225 SEN CNFA
326 SEN CNFC

Name	(PLEASE PRINT)	
Address	Apt.#	
City	State/Prov.	Zip/Postal Code

* Terms and prices subject to change without notice. Sales tax applicable in N.Y.
** Canadian residents will be charged applicable provincial taxes and GST.
   All orders subject to approval. Offer limited to one per household.
   ® are registered trademarks of Harlequin Enterprises Limited.

DES99   ©1998 Harlequin Enterprises Limited

SILHOUETTE® *Desire*

the popular miniseries by
bestselling author

ANNE McALLISTER

continues this summer with

THE STARDUST COWBOY June '99 (SD #1219)
Riley Stratton wasn't any kid's imaginary hero—capable of
making dreams come true. Not when his own dreams had bitten
the dust. But he had to do the honorable thing by Dori Malone
and her son—*his* newly discovered nephew. And when the duo
moved onto his ranch, the single mom made Riley dream...of
things not even Jake's stardust cowboy could make come true.

COWBOY ON THE RUN August '99
(ST—World's Most Eligible Bachelors)
When cowboy **Rance Phillips's** ranch was overrun by a
busload of brides-to-be, this last eligible bachelor left
town...and landed right in the arms of his former flame, Ellie
O'Connor. But Rance soon suspected that Ellie was hiding
secrets...about her oldest son, who was the spittin' image of a
certain cantankerous cowboy!

Look for more **Code of the West** titles coming to
Silhouette Desire in 2000.

Available at your favorite retail outlet.

Silhouette®

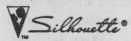